ReSISTANT

Archives of The Monarch: Book Two

ReSISTANT

Helen McMahon

Carpenter's Son Publishing

Resistant

Published by Carpenter's Son Publishing, Franklin, Tennessee

Published in association with Larry Carpenter of Christian Book Services, LLC www.christianbookservices.com

Interior and Cover Design by Suzanne Lawing

Edited by Robert Irvin

Printed in the United States of America

978-1-946889-79-9

Contents

Contents

Prologue

My Dearest Dmitri,

Do not think that your failings will be overlooked. Far from it. I expect better from you. San Francisco was a pet project of yours, I know. But should I find your experimentation to further place at risk this empire we have built, I assure you it will not be allowed to continue.

I expect the citizens of your city will remain in their homes for fear of the Virus. You should thank Joseph Clere for his love of that girl. Had your precious city not been on Lockdown . . . we would have more to discuss.

I cannot express my disappointment in words you will understand, Dmitri.

Nor can I find any statement grave enough to put to voice my anger that you have exalted yourself so high in your own little world. Do I hear correctly the fears of your people? They suspect you to be The Monarch himself.

Perhaps they can be allowed to do so; no harm has been done. But do not think that will be a pardon for you. You have claimed my title. You have rolled it in the mud, doing all the dirty work yourself. Some may call that "old-fashioned hard work." I call it sloppiness.

And you have failed. Unimaginably. With my name at stake.

Forgiveness for such does not come easily with me.

Mend this. I will not ask a second time.

The Monarch

ONE

The Veil Groans

The Veil won't fall. We're still running, and I don't know where. My heart is writhing in my chest, fighting the pain that has been flung at me, forced through my bones. Something else is wrong, and I think I now know what it is.

That perfect, clear blue . . . it is the *wrong* blue. Too bright, too clear. I've seen it before. I was too caught up in everything to notice. But now I do.

We were always told the Veil was a network of glass-like plates held in formation by some advanced electromagnetic something-or-other. That was used to enforce the belief that the Veil was see-through. But we know it is not. If that had been so, as soon as we inputted the virus and the shutdown code, the magnetic field would have crumbled and the dome would have collapsed in on itself.

Needless to say . . . it hasn't.

That is a punch in the gut. Not that I haven't had enough today. I'm not thinking about it right now. Right now, I have to run with everything I have left, which isn't saying much.

But even as we run, something else is happening. The Veil is groaning. We're all running toward the edge of the Veil, but I don't know what we're going to do when we get there. The

Veil isn't falling.

Wasn't. Without further ado, blackness envelops everything. *Everything.* We seem to have fallen into a hole; there is no light filtering through from anywhere. I have seen the dome at night. At real night, not just with the contacts. But this is a wholly different level of pure blackness.

My stomach falls; fear screams heavily into my ears. We all stop. What else are we supposed to do? We can't see six inches in front of our faces! Suddenly, I have the horrible sensation of being totally alone.

I panic. *Adam?* I spin around, trying to see anyone, trying to retain my composure. I know he's dead, but there are no other words I can bring to mind. *Adam?!* I'm breathing so fast. Too fast. "Adam?" I finally say, turning in circles, straining for sight. My head is spinning. "Adam!!" I scream.

He's dead.

"Adam, where are you?" I spin around, seeking . . . anything. "Please, I can't see anything. Where are you, Adam?" I can hear something now, but my mind can't process it. A voice maybe? Maybe more than one voice . . . I don't know. "Adam!!" I scream as loud as I can.

He'll answer me. He will. Somehow, I know it.

From the blackness, I feel two hands on my shoulders from behind me. "Adam?" I shriek and spin around.

"Hey, hey. Devynn. I'm right here." Dekker. My mind snaps.

"No!" I shout and shove at his hands. I can't process this. Any of it. This isn't happening.

He sighs. "Devynn . . . "

"No, don't you touch me!" I yell at him, backing away, nearly falling over my feet. "Adam!"

"Devynn." He's coming toward me again, and I flail at him, spewing nonsense and screaming for Adam. *Who I know is dead.* It's like my mind is divided. Half of my mind knows what is happening and understands what I need to do. That half also understands that I'm acting like a lunatic. But the other half has dominance—and won't let up.

Finally, Dekker grabs me by the shoulders. "Devynn!" he says loudly, firmly, forcefully. I try to wring myself from his grip.

"Let go of me!" I hiss and push him. He doesn't budge. "Let go of me!" I scream and thrash. He flips me, arms locking me in place with my back against him. I groan and writhe—clawing, shouting.

Finally, I lift my feet up and try to fling myself to the ground. A useless maneuver, as Dekker is unfazed by my weight. "Devynn . . . " he says, and I can hear something akin to pain in his voice.

I begin to melt, falling apart. "No! No, let go . . . " Tears stream down my face. My body trembles with rage in his grip.

"No, I'm not going to." The anger splits through me again. I arch backward, trying to make him let go. He won't. He's like a wall. I press back against him with all my strength. He barely shifts to accommodate. I claw at his hands, trying to dig my nails in, to free my upper arms. "Devynn, stop." He says it quite calmly.

"No! Let go of me, Dekker."

"I'm not going to do that."

"Why not?!" My voice is weakening. I'm sobbing. He doesn't reply. I'm not sure he knows why he can't let go of me. I'm not sure I do. Deep inside, somewhere, I'm actually glad he doesn't. I try to free myself for barely a second longer before falling limp against him. I let the pain rip through me, and begin to sob heavily.

Adam is dead. No, he can't be . . .

All I can do is weep. In complete blackness. "Listen to me, Devynn." I sniff, my body shaking, face and neck soaked in tears. "I don't know what is going on, OK?"

I nod. "OK." I try to move my arm to wipe my eyes, but he

still holds me tight.

"We have to get out of here. I don't know how to do that, but I know I can figure it out." He takes a heavy breath. "I can. But these people are scared. They've trusted me this far, and I don't even know how many died, Devynn. They're going to panic. I need them not to do that yet, OK? I need us all to work together and figure this out, because I can't get us out alive and keep everyone calm at the same time. So I need your help. Do you understand what I'm saying?"

I clench my eyes together, my head throbbing and throat sore. "Yes."

"I know what you're going through . . . I promise. I do." He swallows, hard. "But I need everyone to stay strong. Please. We're almost there. I know it."

He sighs, deeply. I do the same. "OK."

"OK." It is now that he lets go of me.

All my weight transfers back to my feet. I feel a hundred pounds too heavy. But I can do this. *God, please help me . . .* Then I am aware of the wind. Like a huge fan blowing on me, but softer. Wind. *But there is no wind inside the Veil.* I know this to be fact. The city had to keep fans on the trees to keep them strong enough not to collapse in on themselves. But this is definitely wind.

I don't think much about that right now. At this moment, the only thing I can hear is the dome groaning. Creaking and cracking far overhead. Dread seeps through my bones. I'm beginning to think there was some kind of electromagnetic reinforcement. I don't even know if anything like that is possible . . . but the Veil is severely weakened.

It creaks again—louder, longer, and closer this time. I hear a few shouts that seem not too far off. Dekker calls out; several answer back. Everything is still so black.

But then I realize it's not totally dark. There is a web of pale light over the whole sky. It snakes around odd corners and forms the hexagonal pattern I have grown to resent and fear. It is a symbol of The Monarch, who has taken everything from me. *Everything.*

The Veil is creaking and scraping, metal against metal. The sound is deafening. I stare up into the white-webbed blackness. Hoping. Praying for something more. I don't know what more. But I definitely need *something.*

That something comes sooner than I expected. A single seam of light widens and widens into a brilliant gash of flooding radiance. The squealing and scraping of the metal suddenly ceases, and a single chunk of the Veil falls.

The silence hangs in the air for an extended moment. We watch, faces lit with the white light streaming from the hole in the Veil. For that beautiful second, I want to cry. Scream out our victory. *Praise God for getting us this far!*

But then that moment ends. The chunk of the Veil that fell is massive, and several feet thick. It falls and rips into the grass and dirt, sending a resonating boom that echoes for many seconds after impact—I'm not sure for how long. The piece of the Veil landed about a hundred yards from where I stand. My heart pounds in the seconds of silence that follow.

I look around and can see the shapes of my friends now. I see Dekker to my left, the blonde head of Varya coming toward him. But nothing I can see now inside the dome matters. I stare into the hole created hundreds of feet above my head. I just stare through it, wishing I could see more. But the light overpowers all else.

The Veil creaks and then falls silent, light streaming down from a single hole; it casts a strange white twilight. I crane to see anything beyond—but there is nothing. Only brilliant white light. I can't look away. I just stare, praying. I want more to fall. I want to be free of this prison. Even if that means being crushed by the falling debris.

I can't believe I am so desperate. But the Veil has settled.

Nothing more falls. "Come on!" I scream, staring up. I hear Dekker whisper the same words and turn to see him staring upward. He breathes heavily, lips moving unceasingly.

"Come on, come on, please . . . God, please. Come on . . . " I return my eyes to the dome. But nothing has changed. My gut churns. My heart hurts. I hear Dekker: "No, come on. Fall . . . " A tear streaks down my face, and I look away from the white light above me. I look at Dekker, who stares; he is still. Finally he closes his eyes and looks down.

He straightens as Varya reaches him. "We're missing at least two people," she says, lowering her voice. "That's not counting Adam . . . What happened?" Dekker turns her away from me and they discuss more, beyond my hearing.

I don't care that they don't want me to hear. Perhaps I would at other times, but right now I don't. Not after everything we did. *Everything* . . . One section of the Veil has fallen, and we're left in this grim twilight until we can think of something else. And now two people—three, including Adam—are dead, captured, or lost, and we can't exactly afford any of them to be missing. We left the facility with thirteen people. A small group and massively unprepared to say the least.

Now we have ten.

TWO

Zachary in Denial

"OK. Who's missing?" Dekker is speaking. I want to know this myself, so I walk toward them. He sees me approaching and doesn't seem to mind, so I join the group.

"Christopher and Myah," Varya says, glancing between Dekker and me.

Dekker sighs, drags his fingers through his hair, and looks at me. "Are they the sort of people who would vanish?" Yes, he seems to be asking me.

I hesitate. I don't know them that well. *But you do, Devynn. Wake up!* "Uhh . . . no. No, I don't think they would. . . . I . . . I don't know."

Varya seems somewhat irked by my uncertainty, but I can tell she's keeping contained. "Would they have gotten lost in the dark?" she asks.

No. I instantly know this, but . . . how can I trust myself to know? I don't have a choice. "No. No, they wouldn't have."

"OK," Varya says, quick to reply. "Then we have to assume they're captured or killed, and make our next move without them." I know she's right, but it sounds horrible.

Dekker clenches his jaw and releases. I'm glad I'm not in

his place. I would be a terrible leader. "Right," he says, and his voice is terse. "But we need more people. Thirteen was not enough. Ten—without Adam and Christopher and Myah—is dramatically worse. I give us an hour, *maybe* two, before fifty officials sweep the dome for us, and we're dead or captured." He takes a breath. "Varya, I need you to stay here and get these guys back to Rendezvous Point. I'm gonna take Serena and Germy, and Benjamin if you can spare him, back to the South facility with me. Once we regroup with my people, we can hit the other two facilities and get the other FCs at least communicating."

I remind myself that FC means First Class. Completely resistant to the Rewrite. Chloe and Dekker are First Class. As is Varya, to my knowledge.

"All right." Varya nods. "You got Benjamin, but he probably doesn't know . . . "

"No. I know. I got it," Dekker says. "Just get them back there safely, and get Eli to make sure the communications still work, OK?"

"All right," Varya says, and turns to the group congregated behind us. It's amazing how small we seem out here in the open. I'm too taken by that single fact to really hear what's being said to them. How could we have done something so great with so few? Or at least it would have been great if it had succeeded . . .

As if in protest of my thoughts, the Veil begins to groan loudly. We gasp and look up, but nothing falls. Bailey speaks up. "Wherever we're going, can we please get there quickly so we don't get crushed by this thing?"

"Yes," Dekker says. He speaks to everyone, but looks at Varya chiefly. "If I can't communicate with you by midnight tonight, then stay put. Do not go anywhere. Nobody knows about Rendezvous, and you'll be safe. If the comms are working and we're still not in contact in three days . . . " He thinks for a long moment. "Then you'll have to reach out to the other facilities without us." I hate hearing things like this. He's basically saying if we don't hear from him in three days, then he's dead, and we have to figure it out without him. I can't bear that thought. So much has been tragic already.

"Move quickly. I expect there will be officials on the lookout soon if there aren't already." He pauses a moment, then goes on. "The light is enough that they can see you with or without night vision, so whatever you do, do it fast." He looks pointedly at Varya. "I'll try to reach you as soon as I get there."

Varya nods. "Good luck," she says as he hurries off toward the Southern Facility. Dread seeps through me as Dekker and his small group leave, but Varya presses us away toward the north as soon as they are gone.

. . . So now we're running again. Half my life now seems to be running. But at least right now I know where I'm running to. Even so, I don't like it. I wanted to be running out into the open air, out into the world, right now, not still living under this awful dome. Instead I'm going back into an underground facility without Adam at my side.

We failed. I guess I should have seen it coming. There were *thirteen* of us. What did I expect? Probably the fairy-tale ending where we get out perfectly and the Veil is stripped away, revealing the perfect day awaiting us. But no. No, we are left to wander in darkness and look for another way out. *Another* way. And it's not like there's gonna be a nice gateway for us to walk through.

The run is even longer than I remember it being on the way here. I hate the dark. I hate running. I hate this freaking dome and I want out! Tears burn my eyes. Tears of pain and anger. *He's dead. Why is he dead? Seriously! Why God?* I wish I could just close my eyes and run from all of this.

Part of me wishes I hadn't even run to the Arc that day. That I could somehow never remember any of this. But how can I say that? I don't know how. But I do wish none of this had ever happened. I would have lived on in my perfect little life, with my perfect job, perfect apartment, and perfect friends.

Well, perfect *friend.* Joseph is to blame for all of this, as far as I know. I don't want to know if Kelly, his cousin, the nurse, knew. I don't think I could handle it if she did. But none of that is important now. I want everything I had back. I don't want this anymore. I thought I was happy and strong enough to do this. To believe. But I'm not. *Forgive me, God.* I'm just not ready . . .

We reach Rendezvous Point and Zachary finds and unlocks the ground door. I wait for a few seconds as the others file down into the opening. Once my feet are on the cement floor . . . I just stand there. A few people move around me. But I hear nothing. The facility is totally silent. Which it never is. The steady whir of the Underground Transportation System has fallen dead. The only light that fills the bunker is a dull green coming from small emergency bulbs. I guess whatever Adam plugged into the system shut *everything* down.

Zachary is looking around the room. He appears to be counting us. Dread and pain grip me. His eyes shift, uncertain. He blinks a few times and scans the room again. Finally, his eyes rest on me. I swallow hard and those stupid, burning tears spring to my eyes again. He inhales sharply and holds his breath. He looks away from me, searching the room over once more. Desperation wraps around him and he breathes heavily, eyes darting about.

My heart aches. He stands a yard or so from me. He looks down at the floor, eyes flickering up to mine, and down again. He clenches his fists and releases them over and over. He studies the floor intently as he speaks. "We're missing three people." He looks up, and I can see the fear in his eyes.

"I know," I say. "Adam is—" He gasps, cutting me off.

"No. It's OK. I know." He holds up his hand to stop me.

"We'll find him."

Lydia comes around from behind him and stands beside him, trying to read the situation. She looks at me, eyes wide, doubtful. "Adam?"

I open my mouth to speak, but Zachary won't have it.

"We've been through this before. He always makes it back." If ever there was a moment when death was preferable to life, this is that moment. I am realizing that Zachary thinks Adam is taken. He has no idea . . . He finally makes eye contact with me. He has to know. I can see it.

"When Adam was upstairs . . . " I pause. How can I know exactly what happened? All I know is what I heard and—and what I saw. The image is burned into my mind. The blood. So much blood. I bite my tongue. "I heard . . . a gun—"

Zachary clenches his jaw. Furrows his brow. "What is it? Just tell me." He stares into my eyes.

My tongue turns to lead. I look at him. The fear in his eyes . . . I just can't speak.

He looks at me, eyes glossy. He swallows and shifts expectantly, preparing himself. But he doesn't know what I'm going to say. How can he know? "What is it?" he asks, and his voice trembles. "Tell me what happened."

"No." I answer, but keep it simple. My voice seems small. Underwater.

"'No?'" he echoes. "No *what?*"

I bite my lip hard. I wish I didn't have to do this. I squeeze my eyes shut. "They didn't take Adam." I open my eyes slowly. Zachary's brow is furrowed. "I tried to tell you . . . about the gunshots . . . "

The blood drains from his face. He stares at me; Lydia gasps slightly. "He's . . . " Zachary's mouth hangs open and his shoulders fall heavily. He looks down again. A long second passes, and Lydia begins to cry. I join her. Zachary just stares. Blank. Uncomprehending. "No." He says it, as with finality. Lydia embraces him, but he doesn't react to her. "No, no, this isn't happening!" He pulls away from her. He looks at her like he's confused about why she's crying. "This can't be happening!" he says, this time even louder.

Zachary chuckles. A nervous, forced sound, but even so, out of place. He takes Lydia by her shoulders. She tries to say something, but her soft voice is drowned by her tears and Zachary's manic denial. He smiles broadly. "Stop! It's not true!" He looks at me, full in the face, without any sadness evident in his eyes. "I'm serious! There has been a mistake, because what you're telling me is not possible." The room is silent except for his fervent insistence. "He's definitely alive, OK?"

Frustration, more than anger, flushes through me now, and through my tears I look him in the eyes. "No, Zachary. I saw him." The image is there . . . constantly. The blood . . . so much red.

"Devynn." He chuckles, and this is horribly out of place. He places a hand on my shoulder. "It's OK. He's still alive. We will see him again. Someday. I know it."

Now the anger comes. I slap his hand aside. "Stop it, Zachary!"

He straightens.

"He's dead, Zach."

Zachary shakes his head, somewhat robotically. Like he *has* to. He *has* to deny this, because to accept it is too much. His eyes are shallow. He doesn't want to listen to me.

"Look at me!" I shouldn't have this kind of strength, but the anger pushes me.

He looks, and I can see a fear in his dark eyes.

"He . . . is . . . dead." Each word stands sharply alone to form its own sentence. My vision is blurred with tears.

He shakes his head again, that same robotic motion, but he swallows, uncertain. "No, he can't be."

"I was with him, Zachary!" I shout. Too loud, but I don't

care; the pain rips through me. Why do I have to convince someone of something I don't want to believe myself? "I heard the gunshots, I saw . . . " I have to pause. I'm weeping. " . . . I saw the blood." In fact, I should be covered in it, I slowly begin to realize. When I look down over myself, I see there are deep, dark stains on my dress, but the green light is hiding the true color. My hands, though . . . for the first time, I'm noticing, the blood on them is still bright. I'm sickened; my head spins. I swallow back everything I can hold in. Which isn't much compared to what flows from me. "Look at me!" I shout again. "This blood isn't mine!" My body shivers. I'm trying to talk, but my words are slurred, muddled by my tears. I hold out my hands. "Look at this!" I breathe in jagged inhales and exert rough exhales, my face streaked with salt and contorted in pain.

Zachary closes his eyes.

I keep shouting. "Why would I lie to you? You think I *want* him to be dead, Zach? I don't know what happened up there! But he's dead! He's gone! I'm never going to see him again and neither are you! Open your eyes!"

He breathes shakily. His eyes open slowly, resting on mine.

"Stop lying to yourself! We have to . . . we have to move on! We have to accept . . . " I clench my jaw, tears streaming down my face. "We have to accept this. That this . . . it happened. He's dead!" My shoulders shake with sobs. "It was in His hands, Zachary! And this is what He did. This was . . . there is a plan here. I have to believe that." I want to wipe my eyes, but I realize my hands have dried blood. I break down. Finally. I just weep.

Lydia comes forward and wraps her arms around me. I fall limp as soon as her warm embrace reaches my heart. I collapse to the floor and Lydia follows me. I just let everything go. The pain, the fear, the doubt, the anger . . . everything. My body shakes violently. I bury my face in Lydia's shoulder.

THREE

Waiting

I fell asleep on the floor. Until about midnight. Now I'm awake, and Eli has confirmed that the comms are working. If we don't hear from Dekker . . . well, we have to. But part of me knows, or just feels, that we won't. He won't make contact tonight. If he does, I'll be shocked. I don't know why. I just have this feeling.

I just finished a shower to wash clean from all the blood. The water ran red off of me. It was sickening until the water turned clear. I don't know how long I was in there. It was probably a long time.

The clock reads 11:56. I flop down on the couch in the middle of the room. I instantly regret that, though because the couch caves inward to meet the springs. I shift and fidget until I'm too tired to care if I'm comfortable. Finally, I sit still and look at Eli, who stares at a black screen. I guess he took the "contact by midnight" thing pretty seriously. But my thoughts are that . . . isn't it totally possible he's just late? What if he had to take a detour to avoid capture, or something slowed him down? I sigh and lay my head back on the arm of the couch.

Tears begin to well in my eyes. As if I haven't cried enough tonight . . . I wasn't even having conscious thought about Adam this time. But I am now. It's a weird thing to regain memories. But as I sit here, they filter in. Thoughts of warmth and comfort. It's fuzzy like a dream, but so vivid. . . . *I'm outside, but my eyes are closed. Adam's hands are on my shoulders, leading me forward. I take tiny steps because I can't see; he urges me to trust him. "You're good, keep going. I got you."* . . . Tears cascade down my face and I open my eyes to seal off the rest of the memory. I don't want it right now. Maybe later. I don't want to think about him at all. Not right now.

Zachary and Lydia disappeared into their room after Lydia woke up, which was a little before me. I hope I don't have to deal with Zachary's denial again. I need him to work through it with me. He's my friend. It's just too hard to have to yell at him about things. Especially something like this. *That his best friend is dead. And that best friend just happens to be Adam, with whom I am in love.*

I sigh and look at the clock. It reads 12:02. I look at Eli and the group huddled around the monitor. Varya stands beside Sha. It's remarkable how much shorter Varya is than Sha. I guess I never saw them next to each other, or just never cared. Even with their height, if I were to see them pitted against one another, my money would be on Varya. Without a thought.

It's so odd how things have changed in just a few hours. Yesterday, just twelve hours ago . . . Adam was leading us. Perhaps more in deed than in word, but he was leading us. And Dekker was here, leading him. Now Adam is dead, Dekker could be, and the girl we knew as Willa in the Western Facility is assuming a leadership role. And the entire Resistant is just readily adopting this. For a second, I'm angry. Why should Varya/Willa lead us? What gives her that right?

Of course, I think this because I'm freaking out about everything. Of course Varya is the best choice of leadership.

She has the experience and training. What that experience includes, I have no idea, but it's clear it's more than any of us can say. And she's stronger. She barely knew Adam, and because of this she's one of the few who have clarity of mind right now.

12:05. If Dekker made contact right now, I wouldn't even consider him officially late. Nevertheless, tension is building, all around the room as much as in me. I don't like this. I don't want to be right about him not making contact. I just want the screen to light up, and for us to see his face on the monitor, with Serena and Germy and Benjamin shadowing behind him.

But the screen stays black, except for a small line of white letters: "Disconnected." The anticipation in the room is tangible. There's a thrumming in my chest. And pain. And an undeniable fear. He could be dead. Or taken. *Rewritten.* If they can . . . And if they can't, then they'll torture him with experiments trying to figure out how to rewrite him. And if they can figure that out, then they'll rewrite him. I shudder. If they can't . . . I don't know what they'd do then.

12:07. Eli mutters something and clicks a few buttons; a loading bar appears and vanishes. The screen still reads, simply, "Disconnected." He runs his hands through his hair.

"It's only seven minutes. Relax," Sha says, tone reassuring. "He'll come through in a bit. Give it time." She scratches Eli's back, affectionately. He bounces his knee, nervous.

If there was any sound at all in this main room of the facility for the past seven minutes, it has now ceased. Everyone stares at the screen.

And we keep staring. And staring and staring. And nothing happens. Suddenly it's 12:15 . . . then 12:30, and I don't know where the minutes are going. Varya bites her thumbnail; this is odd to see from her. Eli bounces his knee some more. Sha rubs his back. The whole room is silent. Waiting.

12:45.

Bailey talks first. "Maybe we should go to bed now."

"No!" Eli snaps. "No. He'll come through."

"Eli," Sha says, looking away, resignedly. "You can stay up and watch it if you want, but it's been almost an hour. If he doesn't reach us tonight, then he will tomorrow. Or the day after. He will, OK? Sleep deprivation isn't going to help anyone."

Eli sighs, mutters an apology to Bailey. "OK. I'll stay up, and . . . and watch. You guys can go to sleep."

I don't want to sleep, really. It doesn't seem like I'm the only one. The others trundle off to rooms to sleep, but Varya and Sha stay up, hovering over Eli. I lay back on the couch and try to sleep. Which is apparently easier said than done.

I close my eyes and can feel the darkness creeping in. The peace of sleep muffling all else . . . and then there's blood. Dark and gushing. Flowing from under the soft, wet fabric of a T-shirt. I startle . . . awake. Barely ten minutes have passed. I sigh and turn onto my side, dozing, only to have the image repeated.

I wake a second time, on my other side, tears in my eyes. I pray. Begging God to remove the image from my mind.

"I will heal you, oh my brokenhearted. I will wrap your wounds in my love. Trust in Me."

I want to, God . . . please strengthen me.

"I will uphold you with my righteous right hand, oh my love. I know all your tears. None of them are missing from my hand."

So I cry. And I have to trust Him to know my tears and remember all of them. I used to want to remember. Now I'm able to remember! Things are coming back. Memories . . . of everything. And now all I want to do is forget them. Or at least fall asleep. For now . . .

"Keep going. I got you." His voice purrs behind me. His

hands rest like a warm weight on my shoulders. "Keep your eyes closed . . . almost there."

I giggle. "Where are we going? Seriously?"

"Shh. Keep your eyes closed. You'll see." I sigh, exasperated, and keep inching forward. When he finally does take his hands away from my eyes, I can't see for a second. It's so bright out. I squint and blink, and finally the image before me clears. I'm standing at the edge of the Veil, behind the trees, under the giant white fans that reinforce them. I look up at them. The blade is swinging around to come down. I gasp and duck, and I feel the wind swoosh over me. I squeal, and Adam laughs as I cling to him.

"It's OK!" he chuckles. "They're way too high to hit you, I promise." I look up, just in time to see another *whoosh* by me. I flinch as it reaches its lowest point, which I now see is at least ten feet above my head. Definitely. Probably more. "Come on." He starts forward and I walk with him until we're standing directly under the blades. "Now look up." He stands behind me and, as I look up, my head brushes his chest. "Don't look away. Stay still."

I laugh and fidget, trying to keep still. The blade comes around slowly, but as it draws nearer to pointing straight down, it seems to gain speed. I grab Adam's hands. "Ahh, this is scary!" I say, laughing as it comes closer.

He chuckles. "Keep looking up." So I do. And the blade flies over me, the rush of wind taking my breath away.

Then I smile. I lean back against him and stare upward, the blades rising and falling over us, the wind in our faces. We are completely at peace . . .

But then I wake—a third time. My eyes open slowly. I'm staring at the gray ceiling. My mouth is dry, like my eyes. One glance at the clock tells me it's seven-thirty. I have been sleeping for well over six hours, but I have no doubt I needed it. When I look around, I see Sha asleep on the loveseat opposite me. I look toward the computer. Varya is asleep in a chair next to Eli, who has his head in his hand, elbow on the table, sound asleep.

The computer screen reads: "Disconnected."

FOUR

Petrov's Doubts

"Ryan." Petrov looks at the young man in the room. "Ryan, can you hear me?" The oxygen mask on the man's face obscures his features. He slowly wakes; Petrov anticipates. His hands shake as his eyes rest on Petrov's. Petrov smiles and swallows. "Hey, buddy." Ryan's breath speeds up, and Petrov pats his shoulder. "Hey, hey. It's all right." He nods reassuringly, smiles gently. "You were in an accident, OK? Everything is going to be all right."

Ryan tries to speak. Only a breathy whisper comes out. "Accident . . . ?"

Petrov nods. "Yeah. Caleb was driving. You and Eliza were in the car."

"Caleb and Eliza?" Ryan mutters.

Petrov sighs. "Eliza is fine, and you're getting there, Ryan. But Caleb is hurt. Pretty badly. We're holding out hope. I'm sure he'll recover."

"I . . . I . . . can't remember."

Petrov smiles, comforting. "It'll come back to you. It was pretty traumatic. I'm not surprised it's blocked."

Ryan seems distressed. "What happened?" His eyes flit back and forth; his breathing through the mask is quickened.

"A car accident?"

The disbelief in his voice isn't confusing to Petrov. Car accidents are rare since there are so few cars. But then, this wasn't technically a car accident. "No, actually. Your car was randomly attacked as part of a riot."

"What? Where am I?" Ryan asks. The monitor to his left beeps faster.

"You're in Russia. Remember? We had a malfunction in the San Francisco sector. The Resistant compromised the Veil. They know."

"I remember that," Ryan says, and his heart rate settles a bit. "But why am I here?"

"We evacuated all Monarch Personnel when the dome shut down." Petrov grabs the nurse's stool and sits beside Ryan's bed. "You and Caleb were in the Capitol with Eliza, so you went to the Underground Transportation System. Remember?" Petrov chuckles lightly. "We couldn't think of a good phrase for U, T, and S, so we always just called it The System. You remember that?"

Ryan thinks hard. "Yeah . . . I think I do." He gestures to the oxygen mask. "Can I take this off?"

"Oh, yes." Petrov stands and removes the mask from Ryan's mouth. "You all right?"

He nods. "Yeah." He blinks slowly. "You were saying . . . ?"

"Anyway, I called you and told you to get to Russia and you did. On your way to the facility there, you encountered a riot, and your car was attacked because of The Monarch symbol on it."

Petrov sighs, but very slightly, so it is only to himself. *Is this fight worth this? Trying to control a handful of worthless rebels when the world is at peace? Can't they just be ended? But no. They are to be rewritten to ensure absolute control. The Monarch is obsessed with control.* Petrov understands that obsession sometimes . . . *But why? The Monarch has most of the world controlled. Why does he require every last soul?* Petrov scolds himself. He knows that *control* is not the goal of The Monarch. The goal is peace. It angers Petrov to think people have been killed for bearing the symbol of that peace.

Petrov's mind returns to Ryan. "It was a terrible thing," he adds, softly.

Ryan furrows his brow. "What is happening? Something isn't right." His breathing elevates, his pulse suddenly skyrockets. "What is going on, where am I?" His monitor begins to emit a different type of sound. Loud . . . obnoxious. "Something isn't right!" Ryan yells.

Two doctors, each flanked by two nurses, enter the room. "What happened?" one of them asks Petrov.

"I don't know." Petrov answers as calmly as he can.

The other doctor quickly takes his place beside Ryan. "Hey, Ryan. What's the matter?" the doctor asks, and now he is looking at the monitor and whispering orders to the nurses at his side.

"I . . . can't see . . . " Ryan says.

"OK." The doctor begins adjusting something, but what he is doing only he knows. "Everything is going to be all right, Ryan. Can you hear me?"

"I'm gonna . . . pass out," Ryan says.

The doctor shines a light in Ryan's eyes. "Nystagmus and weak pupillary reflex." He looks directly at Ryan. "Ryan? Can you smile for me?"

Ryan smiles slowly. Petrov notices how his face seems to droop on one side; dread seeps through Petrov. The doctor says something rapidly and orders the nurses to hurry. "Dmitri . . . " Ryan says, diction slurred—and then his body seizes.

The room erupts. The nurses quickly put the oxygen mask back over Ryan's mouth. That and a hundred other things are going on at once. And Petrov is completely worthless. "Sir, I'm going to have to ask you to go out into the hall, please." The doctor doesn't look up.

"Is he going to—"

"I need you to go, sir."

Petrov walks from the hospital room in a sort of daze. *What just happened?* Everything was fine, and now it isn't. *Ryan can't die.* He just can't. Petrov needs him to be all right. And he will be, Petrov reassures himself. He turns to look back into the room.

It is still a flurry of cords, syringes, gloved hands flying. Orders barked, commands executed. The monitor still blares out above all the noise. A babble of long terms Petrov can't understand.

Petrov stands before the small rectangle window, watching the medical workers intently and thinking about how much the Resistant hate him. *Every* Resistant hates him. Even Varya had. His own sister. *Hated*, in her case. She'd been working with the Resistant when she was taken. But she's probably dead now.

There is the possibility she isn't dead. Petrov knows that. But for now, it's probably better to assume that Taurine didn't lie. Assuming the worst gives him a feel for who he's dealing with. Or rather who he was dealing with. Without Taurine, the Resistant are crippled. Even with Myrus, there's no way their morale withstood what happened.

But then Petrov's mind returns to the one simple fact. The Resistant hate him. With every breath they hate him. And they don't even know him. They think he doesn't care about anybody or anything except power. Control. They think he is The Monarch himself. Chills run down Petrov's spine. He is *not* The Monarch. That power is not something Petrov truly wants. Yes, perhaps there are times he craves the respect it brings—the fear the name instills and the peace it brings after the fear subsides.

He would carry the title of The Monarch with pride.

But that's not what he wants to do.

He likes the dirty work. He likes getting into their heads. In a way, that makes him more powerful than The Monarch. Control all the pieces and the board itself doesn't matter anymore.

But of course . . . Petrov doesn't control all the pieces. He'll never be *more* powerful than The Monarch: the man who *owns* the men who control *some* of the pieces. When you're that man—well, then you own the pieces, the players, and the board.

Life is chess. Sacrifices and victories.

Petrov is looking at a sacrifice. And, in some ways, a victory. Without the Resistant he wouldn't hold the pieces he held. And without those, he wouldn't be in a place to crave the name of The Monarch.

But the Resistant don't know him. He's not as heartless as they think. He's just playing the game.

And sometimes, they are indeed the pieces.

*****

Eli keeps checking the system. It's still fully operational, and we're still disconnected. It's almost noon. I'm frustrated. Eli is distraught. Varya bounces her knee rapidly, chin in hand, eyes flickering between the unyielding screen and the clock.

Time feels slippery. Like everything that happens right now is going to matter, and we don't have time to change any of it. I want to go into my room and cry again. But I don't have time—because it's slipping away.

"Come on . . . " Eli is moaning. He desperately needs Dekker to come through. Which he will. I have to keep thinking this. But the chances are starting to grow threadbare. I don't want to have to go on without him. I don't even think we can.

No. We can't. I look, longingly, at the screen. I don't know if

I can explain how much I want to see Dekker's face right now. Or Adam's. I blink away the warm burn of fresh tears. And then . . . something changes. A loading bar appears onscreen. All the breath is swept from the room in one collective gasp.

A face suddenly appears on the screen. In that instant, I'm sure I squealed—or something. A billion questions flood my mind. One of them, Varya vocalizes.

"Who is that?"

The face on the other end is electric. His hair is dark and messy. But not in a bad way. His eyes are a bluish-green, piercing. They search the screen for a second before focusing. "There you are!" he says, and now all of us can see he is grinning at us.

We just stare at him for a second. *Who the heck is he?* Why is he on the screen and not Dekker? His face gets a little more serious and the image shifts as he adjusts it. "So, here's the deal. Dekker is . . . umm . . . well . . . "

"Is he alive?" Varya asks, seething with impatience.

Confusion registers on the man's face. "*What?* Oh! Yes! Sorry. He's alive. He's fine. He's just . . . not here." There is another collective gasp, as though each one of us finally releases the longest breath we've ever held.

"Well, where did he go?" Varya snaps.

The guy sighs and ruffles his hair. "That's actually a pretty long story."

"Talk fast then!" Varya has absolutely no patience for this, but the man seems to sense that. He cuts to the chase.

"He went east. There was an emergency."

"Why didn't he make contact first?" Varya asks in an instant. I look at her sideways. She might have a thing for Dekker. Not a crush, per se . . . but maybe a thing. The notion is intriguing. Almost funny. I smirk, slightly, for about half a second. It's the first time my mouth has been able to turn upward in at least two full days.

But I want the answer to Varya's question as well, so I turn my gaze back to the man on the screen.

He sighs again; he seems to do that a lot. "OK. I'm Jaxon. Hey. Nice to meet you. I'm here with my wife. She's a Second Class. I am a First Class. She's stuck here with me because we have an infant. Chips in the arms, the whole shebang. Not important, at the moment. Anyways!" He looks squarely at Varya, it seems. I guess I can't really tell. "We haven't had contact with anyone but the East. Don't know why . . . doesn't matter. They sent out an urgent message, with no information in it at all. Again, don't know why, and they've never done anything like that before. Ever. But neither of us can leave. So! As soon as Dekker got here, we sent him off. I'm not kidding. Paige—my wife—barely even let him come inside. Germy and Benjamin went with him, just in case something was actually wrong. Serena came in and is making me do this while she calms down. She's a wreck. I've never seen her this shaken up." He looks behind him. Presumably in the direction of Serena. About a hundred questions swarm my brain. I welcome these queries. None of them are regarding Adam, so it's a relief.

Except now, of course, I'm thinking about getting my mind off of Adam, which is thinking about him . . . I sigh.

Varya furrows her brow. "I thought the Southern Facility was Dekker's facility. You're saying it's yours?"

Jaxon scratches his eyebrow. "It was his. Before he went dark."

Oh . . . that makes sense. Like Varya, I thought the South was Dekker's facility as well.

"He cut the chip out of his arm. Actually, Germy hacked it and made it show his vitals as staying stable, and *then* they cut it out and left it in the facility while they got away. Of course, they eventually figured it out. They scoured the place. Basically, the whole dome—and never found him." He smiles. "Still don't know how he did that, by the way." The pride is evident in Jaxon's tone. "Eventually, they gave up the search and threw me in here. I was married . . . " He swallows and looks down for a moment. His eyes flicker. "Anyways, she found me. And we got pregnant." A grin splits his face wide again. "Little boy. Name's Kuri."

Kuri . . . that name is really familiar. I can't figure out why. I'm sure it'll come to me.

"He's asleep right now."

Varya is agitated. "Did he want you to tell us anything? Did Dekker have a plan? What does he want us to do?"

"Yeah. He wanted you guys to get over here as soon as possible. Since there are two of us over here who can't move, it makes more sense for everyone to come here."

Yeah, except the Capitol *knows* about the Southern Facility. I make myself shut up, mentally. Dekker knows what he's doing. *I hope.* I can't doubt him now. First of all, it's stupid, because he's . . . well, he's Dekker. And second, who else do I have to trust?

"And to run as fast as you can to get here," Jaxon adds.

"Whoa, whoa. We're in no shape to just leave here," Eli protests.

"Why not?"

"Because."

"Because why?" Jaxon's eyes seem to carry a mischievous glint.

Eli flusters. "Because. We, um . . . we can't trust you." He begins wringing his hands. "How do we even . . . uhh . . . know that Dekker came to you, hmm? You could be working with the, uh . . . The Monarch for all we know."

Jaxon laughs and grabs the camera, sweeps the room with its eye. "This look like a Monarch facility to you?"

It doesn't. In fact, it's basically identical to Chloe's facility. Just a lot messier.

Eli frowns. "That doesn't prove anything." I don't understand why he's being so hostile, but then it hits me: Eli has been here for years. Maybe he just doesn't want to leave at all. I look at him. He doesn't look back.

Jaxon sighs, and the image on the camera jostles toward a room to the side. Jaxon flings the door open. "Serena!"

Serena is facedown on the bed. "Hmm . . . "

"Can you please tell your friends they need to come here as quickly as possible?"

"What?"

"They're not trusting me."

She groans, rolls over. "Who is it?"

"All of us," Sha answers.

I'm not sure she can speak for all of us as echoing Eli's doubt, but I don't mention it.

Serena sighs. There are circles under her eyes. She has definitely been crying. She's also probably exhausted. She sits up, groggily, then looks squarely into the camera for a long moment. "You believe him now?"

Eli turns his eyes down, mutters something that sounds like a "yeah." I don't know. The camera shuffles back toward the desk, where Jaxon sets it down and plops back into a chair. He leans forward and drops his head into his hand, the pressure nearly closing his left eye. He sits for a second and looks us over, one by one.

"So . . . you guys coming?"

FIVE

Flight to the South

Vertigo. Constant, unending vertigo. That's all I can feel. The ground will suddenly pitch up and swoop down under my feet, throwing me into the air and dropping me down again. It's painful. My stomach is in knots. I hate this.

Is it grief? I sigh. *Is it fear?* We are about to leave. I hope that's all it is. Fear passes; grief takes time. I have to get my stuff, but there isn't much of it. I pretty much just left as I was. With that same stupid duffel bag. As we leave this time, it's full of other people's things. The bag is unreasonably huge anyway.

We ease the door open carefully, the eerie white twilight seeping slowly in. I'm not sure I'm up for a run in the dark, but there is no other way. Dekker said to come. So . . . we'll come. Varya sighs, looks back down the entrance to the group below. "OK. We just have to make a run for it."

I look back at Moses. I feel horrible that I've mostly forgotten about him lately. But now I'm worried. I hope he can keep up. It's a long run.

"There's enough visibility, so just watch the people around you," Varya says, providing a small piece of comfort. And then, sharpness: "Keep *quiet*. If there's anything I've learned from the Veil, it's that sound travels. Just run until you can't anymore." She pauses, tries to breathe. "Then run a little farther."

We are encased in a breathless silence. Slowly, Varya climbs out of the hole. Then Laura, Allen, Bailey . . . all people I feel horrible for not knowing better. Emma, Sarah. Then Zachary climbs through and helps Moses, Lydia, and me out.

Sha climbs out, and Eli stands for a long second.

"Eli. Come on," Sha whispers, holding out her hand to him.

He looks slowly around the little hole that has been his home for who knows how long, and I see sadness on his face.

Sha looks at him gently. Smiles. "I know. I'm gonna miss the heck outta this place too."

He nods, swallows.

"But we have to move now, OK?"

"OK."

We all sit another second, and then Eli takes Sha's hand and climbs out.

As soon as the door closes, we are enveloped in a silence so thick I'm terrified to break it. I can barely make out faces in the light, and I rely mostly on other features. For instance, Varya's hair stands out the most. She hisses out the direction we'll be running, and for several moments it seems like a terrible idea. We're going to veer to our right, west, and run south, hoping to keep distance from the Capitol. I agree about the distance thing, but it also seems like we're almost pinning ourselves against the dome. I mean, if the officials do come after us . . . we'll have nowhere to run. I don't argue, however.

"All right," she whispers. "Let's go!" We all start off, jogging, heads down. I don't know why we're crouching like this, but Varya is, so I copy her. We're planning to stop in the trees near Chloe's Facility. If we were to try to run the entire way without stopping, we'd never make it.

So we're running. Again. It's like this is all I ever do anymore. I don't even really know why. I've known these people for less than a month . . . In retrospect, thinking of the person who was Anna, this is ridiculous. But regarding Devynn . . . of course I can't deny that I know and love these guys. I just can't believe my life has fallen apart to this extent. Honestly, I think I mostly stayed for Adam.

And now he's gone.

My stomach twists in my gut, and I feel like I'm going to be sick. I grimace and keep running. I can't stop. I look around and see several ghostly figures to my left and right. I can hardly tell who each person is. I think that may be Zachary and Lydia over there, but I'm not sure. I'm pretty sure that one, a few over, is Sha, but I'm far from positive. Eventually, I turn my face forward and follow Varya's blonde head.

I don't know how long we've been running when I begin to make out the trees before us, but my legs ache and I'm panting desperately.

I can hear someone behind me wheezing terribly. Something tells me it's Moses.

I try to look behind me, but I can't see him. And Varya said to be quiet. "We're almost there," I whisper, hoping he can hear.

He continues wheezing and coughing while running behind me.

We have slowed significantly, but we are almost there. I begin to realize that it's cold. Very cold. Colder than I've ever felt it outside.

We're in the trees now, and we stay as silent as we can. Varya motions for us to stay close and low. She leads us slowly forward, toward where Chloe's facility is located. I realize I'm next to her. In the front of the group for some reason. I probably shouldn't be up here in a position with such authority. Still, I don't move.

We keep to the trees as much as possible. Suddenly, I hear something. Varya drops. She motions for us to get down, even though most of us have already followed her example. We're all silent, and the quiet is stifling. But it's broken by a voice. And then static, a beep, and then the voice again.

A Capitol official is guarding the Western Facility. Varya curses under her breath, looks out at the others. She makes several hand motions that I somehow understand, and we disperse, each of us hiding behind trees. We all watch her, and when she moves, we follow. I can hear what he's saying now.

"All quiet. Nothing to report at thirteen hundred hours."

Varya motions and we move, slowly. He'll have night vision, I realize. Dread seeps through me. *He'll see us.* He'll see us! My heart is pounding. It's all I can do not to panic, not to make sound. My tongue is dry and I'm breathing heavily. The door to the facility opens. We all freeze, even though, well . . . we were already frozen.

"Anything?" A face appears from the hatch.

"Nope. Not so far," the first guard says, looking down at the man in the hole.

"Odds are the rats will come scampering home—so stay sharp."

"Yes sir." He sighs and slumps. Bored, clearly. "How's the wife?"

Varya motions us forward—and we creep. Ever so slowly.

"Divorced."

I look behind, filled with fear. *They'll see us. They'll see us!*

"No kidding?"

We make tiny sounds, and I'm sure with each one we'll be heard. But they don't look up.

"Yep. She was always flirting around, but as soon as I looked at someone twice—" He slaps his hands together. "So, divorced."

We're almost past them . . . but we have to get a little closer before we can get away.

The first guard laughs. "Yeah, they can be like that."

We keep moving. We're almost there . . .

"Hey! Do you have anything? I think I have movement."

Varya holds up her hand and we are still. I guess we're hoping we look like trees. My heart is thumping. Flinging itself against the walls of my chest.

"No." The second guard looks around. "I see trees."

"Hmm . . . I thought I had a visual."

"Describe."

I can't breathe. I clamp my hand over my mouth. I think I hear a whimper, and I whip my head around, trying to see who is making noise.

"Not sure. Just . . . movement."

I can't see anything. Everything is quiet now.

"Ehh." The second guard just kind of grunts.

Suddenly, the darkened wood explodes. The first guard is firing his weapon! Varya motions for us to get down, but most of us already have. I hear a few whimpers, quickly silenced, and shouts from the other official. *Adam*. It's all I can think as the thunder surrounds me. *Adam* . . .

The bombardment ends. I am shaking. In a lump. I can't deal with this. Not anymore.

"Report! Justify that firing!" It's the second guard, hollering at the first.

"Just seeing if anything ran."

I'm panting, and I cover my mouth again.

"Are you *crazy?!* We don't want to give away this position if we don't have to!" The second guard is hot, worked into a lather.

"My bad, boss."

"That was stupid! How long have you been out here?"

"A few hours . . . "

"All right. We need to get you in here. I'll get someone else." In a few seconds, both guards disappear into the facility.

"Go! Go now! Run! If you see anyone, stop. But *go now!*"

Varya says all this in a very strong whisper. We run. I am next to her, and in a few strides we make it several yards from the hatch—before it reopens and we stop in our tracks again. The new guard turns, slowly, acclimating himself to his surroundings. I don't know how he doesn't see us. I thank God for helping us. Then he sits, his back toward us! We inch away, slowly. Painfully slowly. One-step-every-three-seconds slowly.

Time passes sluggishly. It feels like hours before we emerge from the trees. When we do, we begin running again, or I guess it's jogging; heads are down. Varya is beside me, panting heavily. We all are. I can hear Moses wheezing. My feet catch on something, and I go sprawling to the ground, biting my lip hard. I taste blood, groan. *Ugh. This is all I need.* Varya kneels and helps me. As she pulls me up, I can feel her body is wet with sweat. It's the same for all of us.

She breathes; it's rough. "You all right?"

"I'm OK. You?"

She nods. "Let's just get there."

I start running again, and now it seems the time is flying. A welcome change from the dragging pace of earlier. Soon we're slowing and looking for the Southern Facility. We stop, holding our knees and panting, dragging air into exhausted lungs.

"Varya?" A voice hisses through the night.

Varya looks up and around, but doesn't reply.

"Varya? You guys out there?"

Who is that? I can't recognize the whisper. It could be Petrov for all I know.

"It's Dekker. Is that you?"

Varya sighs in relief at the exact moment I do. "Yes. It's us. What are you doing here? I thought you went east."

Dekker appears ahead of us, flanked by Benjamin and Germy. What a welcome sight. But Dekker doesn't answer. "Let's get inside, all right?"

Varya nods. Dekker walks straight to the hatch we were

about to start looking for and knocks several times. The door opens and Jaxon appears. "Hey! Back so soon? Everything all right?"

Again, Dekker doesn't answer.

A red flag shoots through me; something doesn't seem right.

"Get them inside." Several people get in before me. When Dekker hands me down to Jaxon, I stand in a small pool of friends. And Paige. She reminds me of Lydia in some ways. Her hair is dark and cut short around her jaw. She has shiny blue eyes and freckles across her nose. She's young, and in her arms is a tiny baby. Probably three to four months by the look of the small child.

I'm reminded of my first time in the Western Facility. And the real first time in the Western Facility, which I can now picture—foggily—in my mind. And the first time at Rendezvous Point. Everything is on repeat. It's painful.

I brush off my clothes and see a strange dark stain on my shirt. For a long moment I just stare, then I feel my abdomen. I'm not bleeding, but the stain looks like blood. And it's fresh. I can't think of anywhere it could have come from. I haven't touched anything wet other than . . .

"Varya," I whisper, and walk over to where she and Dekker are still coming down. I look up into the entrance. "Varya, are you OK?"

"No, not really."

I can't see them well, no matter how I keep peering up, but I can hear them shuffling about.

"Jaxon! Get over here and help me!" Dekker calls out.

I move out of the way; Jaxon rushes past me.

"What is it?"

"She's shot."

I see it then, in the dull emergency lighting of the Southern Facility. Varya's shirt. I had thought it was wet with sweat.

I had been wrong.

SIX

Holding On

"Mister Petrov?" Petrov tastes metal. *Mister Petrov? Shouldn't there be a "Mr. President" in there somewhere?* He turns anyway, faces the doctor coming toward him.

"Yes? Is Ryan OK?"

"Ryan is stabilizing, sir. It's Caleb."

Petrov exhales. He'd had a feeling. "Really?"

The doctor swallows and nods. "Yes, sir."

"All right." He'd hoped it wouldn't come to this. But it has. Now he has to make a decision on a life. "Is he . . . I don't know. What's the situation?"

The doctor inhales, then looks at Petrov pointedly. "He's been on the ventilator—" Pause. " . . . for some time now. And he hasn't shown any signs of improvement. Not to mention the other forms of life support we are using. He's not getting better, sir."

The words sting. Petrov clenches his jaw. "You want me to tell you to take him off."

"Yes, sir. If that's what you want. We can continue treatment, but his recovery is looking unlikely at this point. His injury is extensive." The doctor lowers his head. "I'm very sorry, sir."

"No," Petrov answers, and his tone is terse.

"No?" The doctor looks up, puzzled.

"No. Keep him on." Petrov clenches and unclenches his fists. "I need him to recover."

The doctor nods, avoiding eye contact. "Yes, sir."

Anger flares up Petrov's spine. He hates doctors. They always think life is cheaper than it is. The people they serve are just "cases" to them. They are barely human and certainly not people. He glares after the retreating doctor. *Wait till you go on life support and see if anyone will fight for you,* he thinks. Petrov closes his eyes and breathes. Ryan is fine. And Caleb will be fine.

He believes it. Because he has to.

*****

As soon as Dekker and Varya make it down, the room erupts. Curse words fly, and Paige's baby begins to cry.

I don't know what to do. I just stand there, staring blankly as everyone flurries around Varya, who seems barely conscious. Dekker is collected. His eyes are the only thing about him that appear frantic; he is searching for something. Jaxon is beside him in an instant.

I can hear Dekker saying things. I don't know what, though. Something about Paige? The baby? Suddenly Paige is running from the room, the baby screaming. I stand there, still. I need to *wake up!*

Varya is speaking. "I need you to . . . stop the bleeding." She staggers.

Things are falling to the floor. None of it seems important, though; nothing but Varya. Dekker helps Varya lay on the table in the center of the room.

Finally, my mind clears! Paige is rushing past me, back into the room. I can still hear the baby screaming in the other room. Emma—or maybe it was Sarah—goes into the room to soothe the child. I breathe heavily, even though I still haven't moved. Varya was shot. *Shot.* Somewhere in the abdomen. I don't know how badly.

God, please help her.

Silence seems His only reply.

I step into the thick of it. I have to help somehow. "What do you need?" I ask. I'm not entirely sure who I'm directing the question to, but I wait for an answer. The table is surrounded by everyone who can fit around it, even though Dekker and Paige, who both look like they know what they're doing, are the only two touching Varya. Paige is cutting Varya's shirt off with a pair of too-dull scissors. As soon as the pieces are flung aside I can see the full extent of the bleeding.

There is so much. Too much. Varya's chest rises and falls, steadily but shallowly. I stare at the hole in her abdomen. It's off to the left side and appears to have gone completely through her. There is so much blood . . . I can't breathe. Whatever clarity of mind I had—it vanishes. I'm not even looking at Varya anymore. It's Adam. All of it's Adam. All the blood is his . . . My heart is hammering in my ears. Heat. Heat is flushing my entire body.

Varya's body is shivering. "OK, I'm going into shock."

A new level of chaos is reached. I am being jostled by the group. I don't know how I got there, but somehow I am next to Varya and her bloodied hand is squeezing the life from mine as she shudders. Then she just screams.

"Say something to her, Devynn! Just talk to her." I can hear Dekker, but his voice is so underwater.

I am just staring at her, my hand limp in hers. Her head is flung back, her hair everywhere . . . in her mouth, tangled and wet with the sweat from her pale brow. She groans hoarsely. I think she's trying to talk, but I can't be sure. I don't even look to see what Dekker and Paige are doing to her. There's enough blood for me to know I don't actually want to look to find out. "Devynn!" Dekker is staring at me head-on.

I can't reply. I gape at him.

Then I'm talking . . . with a tongue that is barely my own. "Varya. Look at me, OK?" She makes no sign that she can hear me, and no effort to look at me for several seconds. Then she bites her tongue hard and turns her head to face me. Her eyes are watery, her entire face pale as death, and she is sweating. "It's gonna be OK, alright? We're gonna figure this out and you're gonna be OK."

Varya basically says "liar"—but she does it with several profane flourishes.

I can't help a slight smile, and she almost looks like she could laugh with me. It's a sweet moment shared in a split-second, but soon it is over.

Her teeth are chattering, but at least she now seems to be focusing more on me than the pain.

"But, really," I finally answer. "The wound looks clean and like it went straight through you . . . " I'm making this up as I go along. I have no idea if the wound is clean, and even if it did go straight through her, I have no business telling her what comes out of my mouth next. "It looks like it missed your organs and stuff, and you'll be just fine once they can stop the bleeding."

Varya looks more afraid, more vulnerable, in that moment than I have ever seen her. Her body shivers. She swallows. "Really?"

I know I am totally *lying* to her! I can't possibly know any of what I'm telling her, and the looks I'm getting from Paige and Dekker suggest they don't know the answers either. Neither appear to be doctors, and even if they do have some experience . . . it's just not enough for this. However, I say none of that aloud. "Yes. Really. You're gonna be fine."

Within a few moments, nearly everything has ceased. Varya

lies on the table; she has passed out. She's wrapped in something white, probably a towel, with her hands resting on her chest. Everyone stares at her. I'm surprised she doesn't wake for the sheer thickness in the air as we all watch her. It's as if we're just waiting for her to stop breathing. But she doesn't. Nonetheless, the tension remains. No one speaks. Finally, it's Dekker, and he speaks slowly, steadily.

"We have no way to know if the bullet punctured her organs." The room swallows the dread of the truth.

"No," Paige answers, even though it wasn't really a question. "We'll just have to wait it out and see."

"We can't stay here," Dekker says.

"What?" Jaxon looks incredulous.

Dekker looks at him, then at the rest of us. "We can't stay here. We have a very big problem." He looks at me from the corner of his eye, and then back at Jaxon. Something washes through the room. I can't place it. He looks at Varya, who is still out, and then at Benjamin, who sits on the couch, leaning forward, eyes down, rubbing his hands slowly.

Dekker takes a deep breath and brings his hand to his brow. "The East."

"Yeah?" Jaxon says, taking a slight step forward. "What's up?"

Dekker swallows. Apprehension sends icicles through my stomach. I've never seen Dekker this hesitant. "It's gone," he finally says.

"What?" Jaxon gapes. "What . . . what do you mean?" Sha and Eli look up, eyes wide.

"I mean it's gone," Dekker says.

I furrow my brow, trying to get this. *Gone?*

"Bombed, or something. There was nothing left of it but a crater."

"Did you find anyone? Alive?" Jaxon asks, hopefully.

Dekker clenches his jaw. "No one alive."

"Anyone?" Jaxon swallows. "Anyone at all?"

"Yes. But there was no one alive," Dekker says, trying to skirt the issue.

"How many?" Jaxon demands.

"Jaxon . . . " Dekker sighs.

"Dekker. How many?" Jaxon stares at Dekker unyieldingly.

"Three," Dekker answers. "All three."

"What?" Jaxon is horrified. He drags his hands over his face and groans. "*All* of them?" Disbelief infests his tone.

A long moment drags by, something like fingernails on a chalkboard. Dekker breathes steadily. Then he nods. "All of them."

The air leaves me in a single *whoosh* and my chest aches. I hold out my hand for stability, find the couch, and lean hard against it. The Eastern Facility . . . was bombed? Or destroyed, in some other horrific way, with everyone inside it? What does that mean for us? Is Petrov bombing everyone, everything?

"We aren't safe here," Dekker says again.

"Well, now what?" Jaxon asks. He looks at Dekker pointedly. "We can't leave! Paige and I are trapped here. Even Kuri's chipped. Not to mention *her*." He gestures to Varya.

"Germy can get past the chips," Dekker says. "And—" He looks at Varya. "We can . . . figure something out." His voice is calm, but everything else about him suggests immense stress.

Jaxon looks unconvinced. "For all we know she has massive internal bleeding, which means we can't move her, and they could be over our heads right now." His face has reddened, and a sheen of sweat glistens below his hairline.

Dekker rubs his collarbone, deep in thought, as if he's barely conscious and just trying to form a solution. The situation is dire. We all know it. Everyone can feel it. "We have no one who can fix this?" Dekker says.

I exhale. No one offers anything to cut the silence.

Dekker exhales and a muscle in his jaw clenches.

I look away from him. I can't think of anything. If we had someone, *anyone*, with medical training we could . . . I gasp and straighten. "Oh my gosh!" I say, and everyone looks at me. "Kelly!" The confusion around the room multiplies. "My . . . well . . . Anna's best friend is a nurse. I know where she lives."

"She's just a nurse, though," Jaxon says.

I sigh. "Yeah, I know, but—"

"It's the best we've got right now," Benjamin puts in. "If we can make it there . . . we might have a chance."

"Whoa, whoa . . . go to the city?" Jaxon says. "Are you crazy?"

"Well . . . " Benjamin starts.

Jaxon cuts him off. "You can't be serious." He's looking at Dekker.

Dekker looks at Jaxon for several seconds. Then he speaks. "You have a map?"

SEVEN

Stay or Flee?

"Have you lost your mind?" Jaxon says as we make our way downstairs to the hologram generator. "This is insanity."

He sounds like he's going to continue, but Dekker interrupts. "Let's just look at the map, Jaxon, and then we can talk."

Jaxon grits his teeth and several seconds pass.

My heart is pounding.

Jaxon pulls up a map of the city and steps back, arms folded.

Dekker steps forward. "All right. First things first. Where does she live?"

It takes me about two seconds to locate Kelly's apartment.

"That's at least, what? A three-hour walk? Maybe two if we run the whole way?" Jaxon says, not even trying to pretend he's supporting this. "It's way too dangerous. They'd catch us."

Dekker studies the map, not acknowledging Jaxon at all. His eyes move slowly over the map's surface. I can't see what he's thinking. I don't know if he is trying to figure out how to tell us there's no way we can make it, or if he's trying to figure out *how* to make it. "We can make it," he says finally, with conviction.

Jaxon looks at him, incredulous once more. "Dekker. Look at the map. We *can't* make it. They'll see us."

"I *am* looking at the map. You're not." Dekker points at a street that passes by Kelly's, but it travels at an odd angle. It's barely an alley. It's also quite a bit out of the way. "It'd take longer, but we could make it."

Jaxon sighs, frowns. "Dude, no. This can't be our best option." He looks around the room at all the Resistant. "This is crazy risky."

"But if she can help Varya . . . " Dekker says, letting his sentence trail off. "We can't stay here, anyway."

"I'm just trying to weigh the cost. We don't even know what moving her will do. It . . . " He lowers his voice slightly. "It might not be worth it."

Dekker's eyes move toward me momentarily. I can't help feeling heat creep up my neck. *Not worth it?* The moment Jaxon says it, I know he's probably right. This is a bold move. We'd all be at risk. Still . . .

"I think it is." Dekker is speaking, looking straight at Jaxon. "She's invaluable to us. She's Petrov's sister."

"What? For real?" Jaxon blinks when Dekker nods. "OK, but . . . that won't matter if we're all dead."

Dekker clenches his jaw. He can't argue. "So what are *you* suggesting, Jaxon?"

"I don't know. Something that doesn't involve *suicide,* maybe?" Jaxon says, loudly, and throws his hands up.

"Staying here is suicide," Dekker shoots back.

"What about Rendezvous?" Jaxon asks.

"You think they don't know about that?" Dekker asks.

"They might not." Jaxon tries.

"Then it's only a matter of time," Dekker says, and his patience appears to be wearing thinner. "Work with me here, Jaxon. Do you really think I'd suggest going into the thick of it if we had any other way?"

Jaxon sighs, runs a hand through his hair, and then down over his face. He rubs his mouth for several seconds. "It's still really risky, Dekker."

Dekker leans down over the map again. "I know."

"Even if we make it—which I'm not convinced we can—how do we know she won't turn us in?" Jaxon spits out, frustration and anxiety edging into his voice.

"We don't," Dekker answers. "She might try. But we don't have any other options."

"God help us," Jaxon mutters.

Dekker sighs. "So, we have to get you, Paige, and Kuri dealt with because of the chips. Germy can bypass them, or we can just skip that, take them out and make a run for it. But we have to leave." He yanks a hand through his hair. "We make for the city. Stick together and use the city and its occupants as cover." *Its occupants?* I'm bewildered by what Dekker means. He goes on. "We can't know that The Monarch won't bomb the city. But because of the civilians, it's less likely. This is our best chance."

"We don't know that," Jaxon says flatly, once again trying to dissuade Dekker.

"No. We don't. Like I said, we *can't* know." Dekker looks at Jaxon for so long I'm convinced they're speaking telepathically.

"We need more time!" Jaxon pushes both hands to his head.

"We don't know. Maybe we already have enough time," is Dekker's calm reply. He starts toward the stairs that lead to the bedrooms. "But we can't waste it." He looks at Jaxon. "We need to get everyone down. We have to explain this."

Dekker takes the stairs two at a time and calls loudly for Germy. I turn and follow Jaxon down the main level hall. He stops at the first door and opens it slowly. I continue down the hall, knocking on every door. Most are empty. By the time I finish with the hall, I've found three people. I don't think any of them were fully asleep, but they still look exhausted as they wander from their rooms into the living area.

Eli and Benjamin are the only ones still downstairs. Eli

looks like he's barely awake. Sha must have gone upstairs to get everyone else down.

In a couple of minutes, everyone is downstairs. Dekker runs through the issue at breakneck speed. A few people, especially Emma, ask questions, and more than just a few.

"We have to take the chance and go to the city," Dekker is saying moments later, as he finishes. The air in the room thickens. No one seems to breathe.

"Just . . . march straight into the city?" Bailey asks, slowly. It's her turn to try to put up a final caution. She is trying to comprehend. When she says it like that, the whole plan definitely sounds crazy.

Dekker just nods. "Yes."

Now it's Allen objecting. "You're gonna have to do some more explaining, because that still sounds insane," he says.

"We have no other option. Even if Varya wasn't shot, we couldn't stay here." Dekker takes a breath. "We can't go to Rendezvous Point because they're inches away from finding that place. Also, it's a dead end. We have no easy escape routes if we are found or targeted, and based on the damage in the east, even the basement there isn't deep enough to offer protection." The room is humming with tension and thought as the various members of the Resistant wring their minds through the idea. "And Varya is shot. If we go to Rendezvous, she will likely die."

"So we go to the city?" Zachary asks. His eyes are focused on the ground; it's like he can't look up. He looks terrible.

"Honestly, the worst part about this is the journey," Dekker explains. "The next worst thing is finding somewhere to hide. There are hundreds of places, but no one in their right mind would let us in."

"Except Kelly." Zachary finishes Dekker's thought.

"Exactly," Dekker says. "Hopefully Kelly accepts Devynn fully, and we'll all be in."

"She'll let me in," I say. "Especially if I'm wearing a gas mask or something."

"There you have it." Dekker exhales. "We just have to get there. We have to move fast. We can't stop and we can't make noise. If we are seen, we have to move *faster*—and hide. Once we're inside Kelly's, we'll have protection, food, a cleaner environment, someone who can take care of Varya, and a *chance* we won't be discovered. And at least we won't be bombed."

"Yeah, unless The Monarch decides to destroy the city," Laura says, hand at her chin.

"If The Monarch destroys the city, we're dead anyway," Dekker quickly answers. "That's a chance we'll have to take." Dekker folds his arms, and as the shirt stretches his tattoo is revealed at his collar and shoulder. "We *should* take that chance. We *should* go to the city. But if someone has something to say, or a better idea . . . let's finish the discussion now."

I don't know why he isn't just flat-out telling us what we're going to do. He has the authority to do so, to lead us in this way. At least in my eyes. But he isn't. I guess this really is how the Resistant works. It's not a monarchy. We work together. I feel warmth in my chest. But it is cooled instantly—with renewed grief. I swallow.

I miss *him*. Of course I do.

"So . . . " Dekker scans the room slowly, steadily. "We can't waste any time. We need a decision."

"The city." Laura says it without hesitating. Several people nod in agreement, Zachary and Lydia among them. It doesn't take much time, or much convincing, to get everyone to agree to the city. It's a difficult, but ultimately quite clear, choice. Even if it means a perilous journey.

EIGHT

'On Three'

"If we can, we need to disarm the chips. But if not, we have to take them out." Dekker leans over Germy, who sits at the computer, typing furiously.

"This is Kuri's frequency," Germy mutters. "And here's Paige's. And Jaxon's." Both men look at the screen, hard—for nearly a minute. "Three hours minimum to disarm all three. And I mean *minimum*. With that much time, I can barely make a distraction that will last twenty minutes." He looks at Dekker. "Definitely not worth it."

"All right." Dekker turns to the rest of us, who stand dumbly, clueless as to what we're supposed to do next. Dekker dives in; we need instruction, and here it comes. "Jaxon, you and I are going to carry Varya. She isn't heavy, but we can't drop her. Paige, do you have anything we could carry her with?"

Paige thinks. "No. I don't think so. I'll look, but nothing's coming to mind."

"That's fine. If all else fails, we'll carry her in a sheet, hammock-style." He looks around the room, mind reeling behind his eyes. Dekker's calm in the face of all these decisions never ceases to astound me. "Allen. I need you to do something for me." Allen nods. "I need you to sit outside the hatch. Keep an eye out. Look for anything."

"Will anyone see me?" Allen asks, Bailey nodding beside him.

Dekker sighs. "They'd have to be looking right at you. We can't afford not to take the risk. I need you to do this."

Allen nods and heads for the ladder. He is out in a moment. Bailey looks nervous, but looks toward Dekker for further instructions. I look at him too, hoping I can be of some use, something more than just standing here. "Paige, make sure Kuri's gonna be quiet, no matter what." Dekker says this pointedly. Paige nods and heads out of the room. "Devynn. Go find something to carry Varya with. Laura, help her." He continues telling people what to do, but I'm not really listening. Laura and I sprint from the room. We stop once we're out of the main area.

"What are we looking for?" I ask, feeling slow, thinking, thinking . . .

Laura looks at me, her green eyes thoughtful. "Anything. Think like poles or something we could wrap a sheet around to make a sort of stretcher. Hey, a *stretcher* would be great—if we could find one."

I nod. "OK."

"I'll go upstairs, you go down," Laura says. "Check the basement first. There might be anything down there."

I nod and head down. The door is propped ajar, and I find myself in the room with the hologram generator. It's dark and I can barely see. I scan the entire room. It just seems so empty. The walls are clear, nothing propped against them. I open a broom closet to find a hot water heater, a broom. I grab the broom. It has an aluminum handle we might be able to use. There's also a small coat closet in the adjacent wall. The clothes rack is thick, wooden. I can't wrench it free, though I try. I double-check the room again and go back upstairs at about the same time Laura has come down, two clothes rods, similar to the one I had seen, in her hand. One of the bars is only about three feet long; the other is about five feet, but thin.

"I couldn't find anything else long enough," Laura says. I disregard the broom, leaning it against the wall.

"There's one in a coat closet in the basement, but I couldn't get it free. It's screwed into the wall."

Laura holds up a screwdriver. "Found this in the kitchen."

We hurry down the stairs and into the coat closet, loosening the rod with considerable difficulty. Eventually we give up trying to unscrew the difficult bar and just grab and pull at it, each of us throwing our complete weight against it. It pulls free; we both tumble backward. Pain shoots up my tailbone and I lay there for a second.

"You all right?" Laura asks, standing.

"Ugh. Yeah. That hurt."

"Yeah." She offers a hand and pulls me up. She picks up the clothes rod. It's thicker than the one she found, and only a little shorter. "This is great."

We hurry back upstairs, both of us now panting. Laura goes down the hall while I wait in the kitchen. She returns with a sheet. "OK. How are we going to do this?" I ask, looking at the two poles and the sheet.

Laura looks at the items and thinks. "I think we should use your pole and go like . . . " She starts working, and ties the opposite corners of the sheet around the pole.

"We could always tie it in the middle, too, if it's not strong enough," I manage to add.

"Yeah. Right." She unties the sheet and carries the two items out to where Dekker stands, beside Varya, who's still asleep, but has moved since I last saw her.

"What do you got?" he asks.

"It's not much, but it'll hold her." Laura briefly explains the contraption, and Dekker nods.

"All right." He goes to the ladder and opens the hatch a tiny bit. He whispers a few words to Allen and then starts back down. "It's freezing out there. We need more than just a sheet. We're gonna be out there for hours."

I turn and run to the nearest bedroom, stripping the bed of its coverings, which aren't many. I go to the next and do the same. I find myself waddling back into the living area with an armful of thin blankets. "OK, good," Dekker says. He takes the first blanket and drapes it over Varya, then takes it off and starts again. "Lift her head," he says. Laura is no longer by my side; Bailey called her for something. I lift Varya's head carefully, and Dekker slides part of the blanket under her. We work the blanket gently under her body, lifting her shoulders and legs one at a time. Then I wrap the remaining corners tightly around her, making sure her arms are free. Then we work on getting the sheet under her. She wakes the second time we begin moving her.

"Hey, Varya," Dekker says softly. "You all right?"

Her face is pale, her skin clammy. She moans. Blinks. "Yeah. Peachy." She looks from me to him, and back, a few times. "What are you two doing?"

"We're going to the city," Dekker says. I wouldn't have worded it like that . . . but he just did, so here we go.

She turns her head to look at him more directly. "What?" It doesn't even sound like a question. "Are you crazy?"

The next several minutes are filled with Dekker and I explaining everything we can to her and me trying to get the sheet under her while Dekker makes no attempt to help me because he's too busy explaining. "And your friend . . . Kelly. She's a nurse?" Varya asks.

"Yes."

"You don't know any real doctors?"

I sigh. "No. She's the best we've got."

Varya closes her eyes and furrows her brow, hand touching her stomach lightly. Dekker's eyes move to the sheet and now he returns to trying to get it under her. And then, randomly . . . it hits me in that moment where I know the name Kuri from. Before we left for the Capitol, Petrov called us, and Dekker and he jabbed at each other about a kid named Kuri who had died. Petrov had killed him, or so Dekker said. So Paige's baby is named after this boy. I look at Dekker. As I do, I realize he's barely looking at Varya at all. And when he does look, it's brief, and he never looks at her wound. I don't know if Kuri has anything to do with that, but I'm not sure what I feel when I realize it. Does he think she's going to die? *Is* she?

After a few more moments, Varya stops talking; we now have the sheet fully under her body. I hold the pole while Dekker ties some tight knots around it, and finally he lets it drop by her side. "You good?"

She just nods.

He nods back. "All right."

Everyone stands, breathless, in the living area. We know we are close to leaving. The plan is simple. We're leaving everything here. Everything we stole, which to me seems like a horrible idea . . . but Eli and Germy have uploaded most, if not all, of the information to . . . well, to something. I'm not tech savvy. At all. But we're leaving the hard copies of everything. We have to move as fast as possible because we'll be wide open. There are no convenient little patches of forest to cover us between here and the city. After the chips are out of Jaxon, Paige, and Kuri, we're out. Gone. As fast as we possibly can.

Paige enters the room, a sleeping Kuri in her arms, and Jaxon and she take a seat on the couch. "We have to cut all the chips out at the same time, or as fast—one after the other—as we possibly can," Dekker calmly says. They nod, and Kuri rubs his teeny nose. Dekker looks at each of them. "Who do you want . . . to do whose?"

"You should do Kuri's," Paige says. "Germy can do mine, and . . . " She looks at Jaxon.

"I can do my own," Jaxon says.

Benjamin chuckles. "You could. Or I can do it if you want."

Jaxon eyes him for a second. Then shrugs. "Yeah, all right."

"OK," Paige says. "I need someone to hold him." She looks at her baby.

"I'll do it," Lydia says.

Paige deposits the three-month-old in Lydia's arms, touching his little face tenderly. "You're gonna be OK, baby . . . " Lydia sits and holds the baby close.

"OK," Dekker says. "Jaxon, do you still have those razor blades?"

"Oh, yeah. Of course." He goes to the kitchen and returns with three blades. He gives one each to Dekker, Germy, and Benjamin and takes a seat. He looks at Dekker. "Be careful with him—please." Then drills Germy with a bluish-green stare. "And with her." Then he winks and Dekker chuckles.

Dekker runs his thumb over a tiny scar on Kuri's soft arm. "The chips should be about an inch up from the scars." He looks from Germy to Benjamin and back. "Ready?" They nod. He looks at Lydia. "You ready?" She nods. "All right. On three." I swallow. The razor next to soft baby skin looks so . . . so profane. "One . . . " I'm not sure I can watch this. "Two . . . " They're going to bleed . . . and the baby's going to scream. "Three." Three razor blades sink into flesh; blood starts to pour. Jaxon winces, Paige whimpers and clenches her fist, and little Kuri screams.

"Shh . . . shh . . . " Lydia says as she holds him tight. Very tight. The kid can barely move.

"It's OK, baby," Paige purrs.

"All right, kiddo," Dekker says. "Almost there . . . " He starts digging for the chip in the baby's arm. The little boy screams loud enough to wake the dead, and it sounds as if he can barely breathe in long enough to scream again. Finally, he's just gaping, screaming silently. "Almost got it . . . " The baby's little face is bright red, and his warm yellow blanket is stained even brighter red. "OK. Ready to get it out. Everyone else ready?"

"Got hers," Germy says, gritting his teeth.

"Almost . . . " Benjamin studies the gash in Jaxon's arm. "OK. Got it!"

"All right. Get them out. Now." They each remove a tiny rice-shaped chip from their patient's arm. Kuri's silent scream turns into a heart-wrenching sob. Paige takes him from Lydia's arms in an instant and begins to soothe him. Dekker wraps a strip of cloth tightly around his tiny arm, and then Paige's; Jaxon takes care of himself. "OK. We gotta go. Right now. Let's move!"

The room erupts. People begin piling out of the hatch as quickly as possible; I find myself moving out among a tidal wave of friends. Benjamin and Dekker lift Varya out once Jaxon and Paige—with Kuri in a sling around her—have gotten out. I see them push Varya up, and try to be of help pulling her, but they seem to have it covered. "Run! Now! They are definitely coming already. Go!" Dekker is saying this as softly yet firmly as he can between clenched teeth.

I start to run in the direction he gestured, glancing back as they hoist Varya onto their shoulders and begin running. I turn my face forward. The air is icy! I can't believe how cold it is! And if the guard at Chloe's, earlier, said thirteen hundred hours . . . well, who am I kidding? I don't know what time that would really be here if he was running on Zulu. Time is all out of whack in my mind. It's so cold!

Moses is wheezing again, Kuri is whimpering, but growing quieter, and Jaxon and Dekker are carrying Varya. Who was actually *shot*. I'm still coming to terms with that. I look back and see that they're catching up. Good. I don't know what I'd do if they were falling behind. We can't afford to slow down for anyone. I can't believe we're doing this. We're going to *the city!* To Kelly's house, for goodness sake! We could be seen on the way there, caught trying to get into her house, or turned in after we arrive. There are so many ways this could go drastically south. But we don't have a choice. We've come to this. This is where we are now. Taking risk after risk, because there's nowhere else to turn.

We do, after all, live in a dome.

NINE

Kelly

In just under three hours, the lifeless city looms before us. We haven't seen *anyone*. Dekker and Jaxon handed Varya off to Benjamin and Allen about an hour ago. We have slowed to a creeping pace as we near the alley that will lead us to Kelly's. I'm toward the back, alongside Lydia. Zachary, however, is much farther forward, just behind Dekker. As we near the alley's mouth, we slow even more. Once around the bend, I can see the empty space at the end of the street. No one guards it. As we'd hoped. For once, something went according to plan. I feel—more than hear—a sigh of relief from my friends.

I now see this city, what once was my home, in an entirely new light. I should have seen how much it resembled a prison. The gray color, mandatory lockdown, curfews . . . I can't believe I was so terribly blind. The lies were just spread so thick, I couldn't see that the truth had been completely removed.

"Psst." Dekker has stopped, and he's motioning me to come forward.

For a second, I'm confused. Why would he want me up front? Then it hits me; it feels like my mind is moving so sluggishly. Obviously, he doesn't know exactly where Kelly lives.

Duh. I come up alongside him. I move forward, toward Kelly's street. "Her house is literally right there. I can see the door."

"OK." He nods and motions the rest of us forward. I guide him straight to Kelly's front door, where we stop. Dekker grabs a public gas mask from its place beside Kelly's door. Hands it to me. "There's no way she'll open the door for you if you're not wearing this."

I nod and pull it over my head. The flow of oxygen starts automatically. Dekker and the others clear away from Kelly's tiny porch, making sure they're out of view of her window. I pound on the door. Nothing. Then it hits me: why *would* she answer the door? She wouldn't. No one is supposed to be out. I buzz the intercom. "Kelly? Kelly! It's me." I need a story. *Something!*

The intercom clicks. "Anna?" *Anna.* If only she knew . . . I pity her. And envy her.

"Kelly! Oh, thank goodness. Yes, it's me. Anna. Please open the door. I'm locked out." I try to sound panicked, and it doesn't take much effort. I haven't been looking over my shoulder much, but something tells me I should be. I glance back. No one is on the streets but the Resistant.

"The dome, Anna. It's down! The freaking dome is *down*, Anna!" She takes a shaky breath. "I'm not supposed to open the door! We're on Lockdown."

She's right. In fact, if she opens the door for too long, someone might come to check it out. I'm just hoping they'll have their hands too full to worry about a single home violating Lockdown procedure. "I know. I know . . . But I had to use a public mask, Kel, and they don't work very well. Please. I'm not infected. I've been out here for hours. It's supposed to take effect in, what? How long is it now?"

"Two and a half minutes."

Whoever heard of a virus showing itself in two and a half minutes? The blatancy of the lie is almost part of its brilliance.

I sigh. "See? I'd know, wouldn't I?"

An uneasy silence follows. "Where were you? You've been missing . . . your house. It looked . . . raided. I thought you were gone." She sniffs.

"I'm sorry. I can explain, but *please*. I have a filter warning in the mask."

"I'll have to put you through Decontamination first."

"Of course. Of course." I grit my teeth. As soon as the door opens, I'll have to hold it open against Kelly's will, and we'll all just have to burst in. She'll see us before we can all go through the Decontamination process . . . I return to the present. "Thank you." I hear the door lock hiss open. I look back at Dekker and wave him forward with urgency. He comes halfway up. "We just have to push in right now," I tell him. "*Like right now!*" He nods and moves everyone else forward.

I push the door open and we all rush in. I faintly hear Kelly screech on the other side of the plastic barrier that contains the Decontamination area. Dekker runs for the flimsy plastic divider and makes quick work of it. In only a few moments, we are all inside Kelly's house, the door is sealed behind us, and Kelly is, well . . . detained.

Dekker has her secured in the same way he held me in the darkness when I was freaking out. He is behind her, arms locked around hers. Except his hand is over her mouth. She looks at me desperately. Pleadingly. She's crying and fighting him endlessly. Her eyes look so frightened. Kelly may be bigger and stronger than me, but Dekker doesn't seem to be having any trouble with her.

"Hey. Calm down. We aren't going to hurt you," Dekker assures her, but she doesn't pay any attention to his words.

I guess, in her eyes, we already have. She definitely believes she's infected now. In fact, she probably sees us the same way I saw Adam when I was first in the facility. As zombies. I rush to her and put my hands on her face. "Kelly. Kelly! Look at me." She screams into his hand. This is not helping. "Dekker, let her go."

He looks at me with great uncertainty. "She'll scream."

"Yeah, probably," is all I can offer. She's not going to listen to me whether he's holding her or not. "Give me a few seconds, then you can tie her up or whatever."

He nods. "All right." He looks at me as if making sure I'm prepared for him to let her go. Then . . . he does so.

She falls straight to the floor and begins crawling. I drop to her level. "Kelly!"

"Get away from me!" she screams and rises to her feet. She runs straight to the bathroom, makes it, and slams the door behind her. Luckily, the bathroom door isn't airlocked.

I sigh and knock on the door. "Kelly. Please just listen to me! I won't come in if you don't want me to."

From behind the door, I can hear her begin violent sobbing.

"Kelly! You have two and a half minutes before you know you're infected, right?" She's still sobbing. *I guess pointing out having two minutes to live was a little insensitive.* "It's been at least a minute already, right? Probably closer to two."

She sobs but clears her throat. "You're infected! And now I am too! I'm going to lose my mind! I'm going to die!"

For a second, I almost want to laugh. It hits me how different she and I now are, and that all this began because I was exactly like she is now. Petrified. I realize now is the time to tell her the truth. "I promise you I am not infected. I'm perfectly healthy! Everyone here is. And so are you!"

"But your eyes! My gosh, Anna, your eyes!" She starts weeping again.

"Take out your contacts."

"What?"

"Come on, Kel. If you think all that is true—I'm trying to tell you it's not—you've got seconds left in life, right? What's the harm? Take them out." I listen. I can't hear anything for several seconds.

Finally, Kelly speaks up. "They're out. What was the point of that?" She sniffs, and I can hear her move to the door and sink down in front of it. "I'm going to die anyway."

"You don't think it's been two and a half minutes yet?" I wait for her response. I've always known Kelly to be very mathematical. And she has an internal clock more accurate than most alarms. She knows it's been at least three minutes, probably more like five. She's just coming to terms with it.

"It must be," she mutters.

I look behind me, back around the rest of the room. Varya lies there, either asleep or just very still, on Kelly's couch; she is still wrapped in blankets. Everyone stares at me and the door Kelly is hiding behind. We are counting on her, I suppose. And I'm probably the only one who can get through to her.

Which means they're counting on me.

I take a breath. "It definitely has been." A long pause. "Kelly, you're still alive, right? Now trust me on this. Can I come in?"

"No."

I sigh. "Why not?"

"You're infected!"

"If I was, wouldn't you be?"

"I don't know!"

I can't help a slight smile now. "Kelly. You know how this stuff works. I'm not infected. Neither are you. That proves that none of us are. Please just come out."

I hear her standing on the other side of the door. Anticipating her perhaps opening the door, I do the same. The door opens a crack and she peeks out.

I lean so our eyes are parallel to each other, and then I smile. "See? My eyes are still hazel, right?"

She peers around me, just stares at everyone else. "What ... happened? You were all infected! I ... I saw you!" She opens the door a bit more. Only about an inch or two, it seems. But her voice is calmer.

I smile. "I know. It's a . . . Kelly, it's kind of a long story." I put my hand against the door and push it open a little more. She doesn't try to close it, and I can see her whole face now. "Hey," I say, trying to sound reassuring. Or something.

"Hey." She's shivering, adrenaline probably. She looks around me, toward where Varya lays on the couch. "Who's that?" Her wide eyes flicker back toward mine. "Is she dead?"

I bite my lip. "Kelly, she's why we're here. She's, um . . . " I turn and look at Dekker, really not sure what I'm going to say. "She was shot."

Kelly furrows her brow. "And you want me to . . . what?"

"We don't know. Whatever you can do." I look down and blink a few times. "She's my friend, Kelly. If you could . . . just try?"

She clings to the door and eyes Dekker suspiciously. "These are your friends?"

I smile and chuckle softly. "Yeah. Like I said, it's a long story."

As she steps through the doorframe, it's like she's walking on eggshells. She literally tiptoes to the center of the room, trembling. We all barely breathe, and I'm not sure why. Dekker's eyes flicker to Varya and then to me, then rest on Kelly. We're all anticipating what will happen next. Varya's life hinges on it.

Kelly peers past Allen and Bailey and sees Varya on the couch. Then she starts to walk into the living room and everyone clears a path. I notice just now that Varya is awake, but she looks terrible. Her face is clammy and her trembling lips carry a purple tint.

She looks at Kelly, appraises her. And who can blame her? Her life rests in this woman's hands.

Kelly seems to switch modes and drops to her knees beside Varya. "Hey. My name is Kelly."

"So I hear." Varya swallows. "Varya."

"Varya." Kelly tries saying it. "OK. Nice to meet you. Do you mind if I take a look?"

For a second I'm sure Varya is going to say something sarcastic or even witty, but she doesn't. She just nods her head.

Kelly begins to peel the blankets away, and finally Varya's cut shirt. She furrows her brow but makes no other sign that she's disturbed by the amount of blood. But I am, so I swallow and turn away . . .

There's got to be something useful I can do, so I wander into the kitchen. I can hardly remember the last time I ate something that I actually cooked. Could be a good thing, since I'm not a very good cook. I can make a mean cup of coffee, but I'm pretty sure none of us need caffeine right now. I nod to Dekker and Jaxon, who stand on opposite sides of the island in the center of the tile floor.

Jaxon sighs. "What now, Dekker?"

I try not to appear like I'm listening to their conversation, but I am. I find myself opening Kelly's cupboards.

"I don't know," Dekker says with brutal honesty, his voice heavy with fatigue.

"We gotta get out of here," Jaxon says. "If The Monarch wants to salvage this mess, they'll have to evacuate the citizens. It won't be long before we have nowhere to hide."

He has a point, but I try to focus on what I'm doing. Kelly has four boxes of spaghetti, and I bring them all down. Her fridge contains tomato sauce, so that comes out too.

"I know that," Dekker replies, voice low. "I'm trying. I don't know what we're going to do. I got nothing. I don't want that to freak anyone out, though."

The way he says it sounds like he's hoping I don't hear him, so I pretend not to. I'm just cooking. I'm cooking because I'm nervous, probably, but a warm meal can't hurt either. Especially after that freezing run. But what they're saying does have a nagging feel to it. We *don't* know what to do next. We *can't* stay here forever, and we have *nowhere* else to go. I swallow hard past the lump in my throat.

Lydia steps into the kitchen beside me, and the hushed conversation behind me ceases. "Spaghetti?" she asks, a soft smile.

"Yeah. Four boxes. Think it'll do?"

"Unless Zachary insists on eating a full one." She smiles, but it quickly fades. "Actually, he's probably not hungry."

I sigh. "I'm not really hungry either." Regardless, I fill the biggest pot I can find with tap water, which is probably treated with some horrible chemical. I put the pot on to boil, hoping we won't get poisoned. I lean against the counter adjacent to the stove and look at Lydia. I see the tense glances between Jaxon and Dekker from the corner of my eye.

Lydia leans against Kelly's large kitchen island and faces me. "Are you OK?" she asks softly.

I look at the floor. No, of course I'm not OK. Adam is . . . I clench my jaw and let myself think the word. He's *dead*. I look up at Lydia, who smiles a poignant sort of smile. My eyes burn with tears. Time to be honest. "No. No, not really." I can feel myself breaking apart. Lydia's misty eyes aren't helping.

I sniff and look up to stop myself from crying, but it's utterly useless. The tears spill over and I lower my head. I don't say anything, and neither does she. I want to ask her if she's OK, because that's the nice thing to do, but right now . . . right now I just need to cry silently.

So I do.

Eventually, though, the water boils and I drop in all the pasta. I wipe my eyes and make a halfhearted attempt at a smile in Lydia's direction. She comes forward and hugs me. When we pull apart, she sighs. She looks like she wants to say something, but there really is nothing to say. So we just stand there, looking at each other, fully understanding each other's pain. As much as we can, anyway. Dekker and Jaxon are awkwardly trying to ignore us.

A few moments later Kelly enters the kitchen and gives me a look I don't want to see. She swallows. "The wound is, um . . . well, it's pretty clean. No shredding or anything. She lost a lot of blood." Her eyes flit uncertainly from Dekker and Jaxon to me. She draws her shoulders up, shrinking herself. "I don't have any resources at the moment. There's . . . very little I can do."

Dekker sighs lightly and rubs his forehead with his right hand. Jaxon slumps. I just stand there because I don't know what else to do. Lydia shifts her weight.

Kelly raises her eyebrows and looks down. "I can make sure she doesn't get an infection. Uh . . . I can seal the wound and stop the bleeding, but if she has any severe internal injury, then . . . " She shakes her head. "Then I'm useless."

Dekker nods. "How long will it be until you know if she has internal injuries?"

"That depends." Kelly glances behind her. "So far the only symptoms I've seen have been trauma and blood-loss related. So . . . she might be OK."

"OK. Thank you." Dekker nods and glances at Lydia and me before leaving the room. Jaxon follows.

A thoughtful silence hangs in the kitchen, but it's broken by the sound of water hissing on an electric stove. I turn down the heat and open the lid with a dishcloth.

"Thank you so much, Kelly," Lydia says behind me. "You have no idea how much this means." She pauses. "I'm Lydia, by the way."

"Nice to meet you."

I smile at Kelly, who looks at me wide-eyed. "How are you holding up?" I ask her.

She takes a few steps past Lydia and toward me. "Anna, who *are* these people?" Her voice is hushed, but also clearly quite panicked. "Where have you been?"

Lydia looks over her shoulder at me, eyes searching mine.

Kelly is my friend, but at the moment I don't want to explain all this to her. I just want to focus on the noodles, as silly as that is. I try to convey all of this to Lydia through my eyes.

"Hey, Kelly," Lydia says softly from behind her. "Why don't you come sit over here with me, and I'll explain everything."

Wow. I guess telepathy is real. I nod reassuringly to Kelly. "Go on. She'll definitely explain it better than I can."

Kelly swallows and nods nervously. She goes into the attached dining room and Lydia begins to talk. I could probably hear everything if I wanted to . . . but truthfully, I just don't. I stir the soft noodles. A couple of minutes later, as I'm draining them, I hear Kelly's incredulous voice cut through the house.

"What?!"

I smile. She's in for quite the surprise.

TEN

Progress

Ryan is screaming.

"Ryan! Ryan, look at me!" Petrov says. "Just breathe, Ryan. You're going to be all right."

"OK . . . " Ryan groans. "OK." He's sweating profusely.

"This is just therapy. I know it's stressful, but it's really the best way, all right?"

Ryan nods, eyes unsure and frightened.

"OK." Petrov nods and puts a hand on Ryan's arm. "Now, do you remember the attack on Caleb's car?"

Ryan closes his eyes tightly. He looks up, the veins in his neck bulging. "No! No, I can't remember!"

"That's OK. Do you know who Caleb is?"

Ryan groans loudly. "No! I don't know who that is!"

Petrov bites his tongue. "It's OK, Ryan." He swallows and looks at the screen showing Ryan's vitals. He can't push him much harder. "All right, Ryan. Something easy. Who am I?"

Ryan relaxes a little, looks into Petrov's eyes. "You're, uh . . . Dmitri. President Dmitri Petrov."

Petrov smiles. "That's right. Good. Now, who are you?"

Ryan takes a slow breath. "Ryan Watson."

"OK. Do you remember Eliza?"

Ryan's heart rate rises. His forehead wrinkles and he shakes his head, eyes flitting back and forth. "No."

"OK. OK. OK . . . That's all right." Petrov speaks as calmly as he can. "It's OK. Don't worry about it. It'll come back to you. I'm sorry to bring that up."

"It's fine." Ryan adjusts his gaze to look straight ahead. Then his brow furrows. He looks inquisitively at Petrov. "Do I know someone . . . named Devynn?"

Petrov tilts his head. "She's . . . a pretty prominent Second Class Resistant . . . "

"Hmm. Maybe that's it." But Ryan doesn't look sure.

Petrov smiles as sincerely as he can. "What else could it be?"

* * * * *

Petrov loosens his tie as he walks down the hall. *Devynn Wildhem.* She is back to haunt him. He'd known risking so much for her was stupid. He hadn't been taking anything seriously. He'd overestimated the power of the Program; he had been reckless. Now he is paying for it. She is the only weakness manifested thus far in the Genesis Program. *Her.* A stupid Second Class. Petrov can't believe he let it get so bad.

He rounds a corner and pushes open a swinging door. "Petrov, Dmitri," he says to an empty room. He puts his hands on his hips as he waits. The black screen hums to white. "Requesting permission to raise Patient Zero-Zero-One's dosage by fifteen percent, sir."

A cursor appears on the screen; Petrov sighs. Sometimes he gets a voice, but clearly Someone isn't in an obliging mood today.

Reason? The word displays quickly across the screen.

"Patient is exhibiting organic recollections." He puts his head in his hand.

The cursor quickly moves. *Recollections of?*

Petrov swallows his pride. "Another Resistant . . . sir."

Wildhem?

Petrov hesitates, but knows he must answer. "Yes, sir."

Dmitri. I am disappointed, to say the least.

Petrov swallows.

You put an untested program at risk. And for what?

Petrov has no response. His actions were ridiculous. So bad he can't even give a possible explanation for it.

For what, Dmitri?

Petrov swallows; he knows he must continue. "I don't know, sir. I was reckless and overconfident. But . . . " He thinks hard. "But I can fix this. I will prove Genesis using this patient. This is just a hiccup, and I . . . " He stops because the screen is producing new words.

Permission to raise Patient 0-0-1's dosage by 10%.

Petrov exhales. "Thank you, sir."

Patient 0-0-2?

"On life support, still."

0-0-3?

"She's recovering nicely. Haven't started her on the serum, but—"

Pull the plug.

Petrov blinks. "Sir? Three?"

Patient 0-0-2.

Petrov stands with his mouth open. "Sir . . . "

Immediately.

Petrov hangs his head. "Yes, sir."

The facilities?

"All gone, sir."

Did you locate their Rendezvous Point?

"Yes, sir. The trackers embedded in what they stole led us there. It's gone, too." Pride wells up in Petrov's chest. Just a little. He's done something right for the first time in a while.

Confirmed deaths?

The pride deflates, and more than a little. "Twelve, so far. From the East and the North."

West and South?

Petrov swallows. "I haven't heard any news on them yet."

And Chloe Allison?

"She's dead." Petrov smiles. But then remembers he's probably still on the hook for that.

I suggest you make sure of that.

And then the screen goes immediately black. Petrov stands, confused. Allison is dead . . . *isn't she?* He marches from the room as fear courses through his mind. He has lost the confidence of The Monarch. The favor that brought, and with it the breathing room, has evaporated. But he'll fix it. He will.

To start with, Ryan will never remember.

*****

Joseph startles awake when an alarm beeps on the screen. Since he's in Russia, there's really no reason to keep tabs on San Francisco. None that he cares to share, anyway. The notice says that a door in the city had been opened despite Lockdown. It was quickly closed, however, so the person on duty back in the Union marked the issue as resolved.

Joseph straightens. The alarm is nearly an hour old. How long has he been asleep? He wipes his eyes and squints at the screen. Realization spreads over him. The alarm says the address of offense was Kelly's. Joseph looks behind him. No one is watching him. *Good.*

He sighs. He's paranoid. He clicks around for a few minutes and is eventually rewarded with video footage of Kelly's place. There is a woman knocking. *It's Anna.*

Joseph shakes the thought away and fast-forwards the image. His breath catches tightly when he sees a group of people burst into Kelly's door. He rewinds to the single woman, trying to get a look at her face. He doesn't get one, but he's sure. It's Anna.

Now he freezes the image on a shot of the first man to enter Kelly's house after Anna, and this reveals a face Joseph knows well.

The face of Dekker Myrus.

Joseph sits back and covers his mouth with his hand. Anna is alive. That is more relief than he can explain. *And she's with Dekker Myrus. That's a problem.* He also happens to know where she, Myrus, and the rest of the fugitive Resistant are hiding. *That's a big problem.*

He looks behind him again and satisfies himself that he is not being watched. He glances at the video cameras in the room but knows they won't be able to see what he is doing. He swallows and puts his fingers to the keys.

Nearly ten minutes later, the footage is erased, the door opening logged as an accident, and the alert archived. Joseph wipes a line of sweat from his hairline. Swallows past a dry, tight throat.

What have I done?

ELEVEN

JAC1895

What is the endgame? I don't understand the point of any of this. All we're trying to do is to stay alive, but we don't understand why The Monarch has done all of this to us. How can we understand? There's no way.

I sit on Kelly's couch, looking at Varya, a half-empty bowl of lukewarm spaghetti in my hand. She breathes steadily, and her distress seems to have lessened, because when she's awake she no longer shivers. Dekker and Jaxon hover uneasily at the edge of the room, their voices not carrying far. I look over at them, but neither give any indication they're aware of me.

Dekker's face is in troubled thought, his eyes down. Jaxon has a look of urgency and agitation. Allen, Bailey, Benjamin, and Sha are out here, not doing anything. Lydia and Kelly are still in the dining room. Zachary, Moses, Eli, Emma, and Sarah are all in the room behind me, on the sofas, watching TV. Serena, Germy, Paige, and Kuri are somewhere else, but I'm not sure where. It's been a while since I've been here.

The hum of the TV is heard through the whole house, though softly. News. Announcements. Claiming that we should stay inside at all times and that the problem is being assessed. *"Remain calm and keep doors closed."*

As much as I know the falsehood of everything being thrown at us through the airwaves, I also know that as long as there's news running, it means The Monarch wants to salvage the city. That means evacuation . . . is inevitable. I look at Jaxon, whose voice is basically conversational now.

"What are you saying?"

Dekker clenches his jaw, clearly irritated. "We have to stay here for now."

"Really?" Jaxon says. "That's the plan?"

Dekker doesn't reply.

"In case you've forgotten, there's security cameras everywhere." Jaxon gestures broadly. "They probably *know* we're here."

"Maybe they do," Dekker says, his voice still quieter than Jaxon's. "What do you want me to do about that?"

Jaxon exhales—hard—through his nose.

I'm interrupted from watching this scene. "Excuse me?" a voice says.

I jump a little and turn to see Eli standing behind me, wringing his hands.

"Sorry. I didn't mean to scare you. If . . . uh . . . if I scared you." He blinks a few times. He looks more nervous and unsettled than I've ever seen him.

"No, it's fine. What's up?" I realize how stiff I am and stretch my arms a little.

"I, uh . . . was wondering if you knew if Kelly had a computer." He pauses. "And . . . and . . . if you knew where it was and if I could, uh, use it. For intel." He swallows as if this is the most difficult interaction he's ever engaged in.

"Uh, sure. I think I know where it is. Let me just ask." I smile and get up, walking over to the dining room, where Lydia is, even after almost an hour, still explaining the whole story to Kelly.

"Knock knock," I say as I walk around the corner in the

kitchen to the dining room.

Lydia stops talking and turns to face me; Kelly just adjusts her eyes. Her mouth is slightly ajar, and I'm not sure what to make of her expression.

"How's it going?" I ask cautiously.

"Good." Lydia replies with a nod.

"Oh, good." I swallow and direct my gaze to Kelly. "Eli, uh . . . my friend . . . was just wondering if he could borrow your computer?"

She blinks. "Oh, um . . . yeah, sure. That's fine. Do you know where it's at?"

"I think so. Thanks. Same password?" I say it with a small wink.

She smiles. "Yeah." The password is the name of a screen-crush we shared years and years ago. Feels like a distant dream.

"Thanks," I say again, feeling awkward. I leave the dining room as Lydia's voice resumes, only for it to be muffled by the sound of the television and Jaxon's voice as I pass by on my way up the stairs. Upstairs is Kelly's bedroom, and next to the bed is a desk on which sits a thin laptop. I snatch it up and head back down the stairs, unlocking the computer and depositing it in Eli's waiting hands.

He mutters something—probably a thank you—and sits at the coffee table. "Let's see what we got."

I watch him for a moment. "Are you . . . sure that's safe?"

He looks at me.

"I mean, can't this be traced or monitored or something?" I gesture to the laptop. After all, it's just Kelly's personal computer.

"Uh . . . it can, but don't worry. I've got it covered." He nods and goes back to whatever it is he's doing.

I'm sure he's perfectly capable. I let myself relax.

Dekker and Jaxon stop bickering when Eli's fingers begin flying furiously, and Germy enters the room shortly after that.

I imagine the sound of the lightning fast keystrokes drawing him in like a fly to sugar-water, or something like that, but I'm really not sure why, and the image fades. Dekker walks over and looks at the screen, but Jaxon doesn't. He stands stubbornly right where Dekker left him, sending a clear message: Whatever conversation they were having isn't over.

Germy peers over Eli's shoulder and nods approvingly a few times. "Nice."

Eli doesn't look up, but says something to Germy that literally sounds French. Or maybe German. Whatever it was, I didn't catch a word of it. But it seems Dekker did, and he looks up.

"Really? We got that?" Dekker says, stepping up behind Eli and opposite Germy. I finally realize they're going over the information in the files we stole. My interest piques.

"Yeah," Eli says with a smile. "We got a lot more than that." He makes a smug face and clicks once with the touchpad. Germy lights up instantly and Dekker leans in, peering at the screen.

After a few seconds his face lights up as well. "Is that . . . what it looks like?"

"Yeah. Yeah, I think it is," Germy says, face almost literally aglow.

My mind is running rampant and I stand up to see for myself. Once I can see the screen, however, I see nothing but lines of code. I try to read them, but numbers and letters shouldn't even be next to each other. Ever. I did not do well in algebra. This looks like another language. "What is it?" I say before I can try to think my way through this and end up exploding my brain.

Eli and Germy both start explaining it at the same time, pointing, Eli with the cursor and Germy with his fingers, both pointing at groups of letters and numbers running together. I was hanging on. Understanding a bit . . . and then I fell to my death. Lost them; utterly lost. I stare at them blankly.

Dekker has stilled, but he answers, rescuing me from my complete confusion. "It's a kill order."

"For what?"

"For the eyes and ears of this whole Veil," Eli blurts out, clearly so excited he's bursting. "This will blind The Monarch. Completely. They won't be able to see where we are, what we're doing, and it'll basically fry their communications and jam any signal they try to send in."

At that, Jaxon hurries over. So that's one problem solved.

"Why does this thing even exist?" Dekker asks. "And why was it in the Capitol?"

Germy is frozen.

Eli isn't. "I don't know, but now we have it! This is the jackpot!"

Dekker looks sideways at Germy, who is studying the code. "Are we sure about this?"

Eil looks confused and looks back to the screen himself. After several seconds of tense silence, Germy sighs.

"I don't know why it was there, but . . . it seems like, basically . . . " He points to a line of code, then lowers his hand. "It looks like this part right here is . . . "

Eli looks at it and scoffs in disbelief. "What? That doesn't make any sense."

"What are we looking at?" Jaxon asks.

"This whole code is . . . it's useless. It doesn't do anything," Germy says. He looks at Dekker, puzzled. Cocks his head.

I feel like my confusion has spread, at some level, around the room, as now everyone is staring, either into space or at each other, completely bewildered. A completely useless code—in the Capitol? It's so randomly weird that there has to be some other explanation. Germy has leaned in closer and is now literally tracing his finger along the lines on the screen. "This right here. . . . This is the reversal order. It basically undoes everything that the rest of this, up here"—he points with his finger—"had just done. It doesn't make any sense."

"Can we rewrite it?" Eli asks, looking closer at the screen.

As is Germy. "No, we can't. See, look at this—" He points.

"Oh, yeah. . . . Hmm." I look at Dekker, hoping to see that I'm not the only one miles behind this conversation, but that doesn't seem to be the case. I look back at the screen, and still I can't decipher a thing.

"Do we know who wrote it?" I ask, though I'm not sure why that question popped from my mouth. It doesn't really matter, does it?

"Uhh, there is a signature," Eli says, exiting the code and going to the closed file, which reveals the symbol of The Monarch and a line of letters and numbers that don't make sense to me. Until I see, attached to the end of the signature, three letters and four simple numbers:

JAC1895

I gasp and point. "Look at that!" I practically shout, and everyone leans in closer. Germy and Eli's heads are basically touching, and their noses are inches from the screen. It's a little comical, but I push by them to point at the sequence. "JAC!" I say. "That's Joseph Alistair Clere!"

"OK," Eli answers. "Why would you think that? J, A, and C could appear in, uh . . . a dozen places throughout the code. It could be . . . it could be completely meaningless."

I shake my head. "Yeah, it could be. But look at the numbers!" They move in closer and I almost laugh at them. Do they need glasses or something? To avoid laughing out loud, I continue my thought. "Familiar to you, Eli?"

"Ohh . . . " he says after a second, realization dawning. "Oh!" He turns and looks at me, bonking his head against Germy, who is still looking at the numbers trying to determine their significance. "That was the, umm . . . the . . . "

"The code that got you past the security firewall!" I smile.

He does too. But then his smile fades back to confusion. "But why do you think it's Clere?"

I go through the story again. "Because a few days before I came back to the Western Facility I had a random pile of cash on my table that equaled exactly eighteen dollars and ninety-five cents." I pause. Dekker's eyes move to mine and then back to the computer. "I didn't remember putting it there," I continue. "So maybe Joseph . . . is the one who did, giving me some sort of code."

"Isn't that kind of a big leap?" Jaxon says. "Why would he do that? Why would he assume you'd make the connection?"

I shrug and shake my head. It is a huge leap, but these four numbers have been a loose end in my mind since the day I spent that cash. And *JAC*—it just fits.

"Look at this," Dekker says, and he points at a random strand of numbers. Gosh. I feel like I am completely alone in my lack of understanding this entire subject. "This whole thing is new. Brand new," Dekker says.

"Wow, yeah," Eli says, turning to look at Germy. "It looks like it was uh . . . maybe, um . . . it looks like it was recently added. Like, umm . . . *after* we stole the file it's in. That's very odd."

"Here. Move over," Germy says, and Eli surrenders the space in front of the computer. Germy reopens the code. "We assumed that if you removed the reversal code the rest of code would dissolve, but . . . " His fingers are flying faster than I've ever seen anyone's. Even Eli's. "But—if this code is . . . " He zones out for almost five full seconds; the silence is broken only by his fingers on the keys. "What if it's *not* a code?" he says, pressing a final key with vigor.

The code starts to dismantle, and my eyes can't seem to focus on any of it. But even as I stare, pieces of it start to make sense. Words. Like *real words* are forming. We all lean in closer. It seems I have forgotten how silly they looked as I am doing the same thing right now. The words are obstructed by misplaced slashes and wayward numbers, but otherwise it comes out clear as a bell—a direct, intended message.

Addressed, I should have known, to me.

Devynn//
Hope th97 message reac66 you. Im so/rry for ever00thing th/t Ive don5e to y/ou, and the people you care00907 about. I won't h||de the fact that most 88hn the horrors you've endured 00101have been my fault. Because I thought I love3d you, I did things that cannot be ||forgiven.
But I want to 995631. I can see now that I was 000190101terribly wrong. So now I'm here 090801 to make = it right. P7788h trusts me. + The M00101100onarch is close.= Care///ful. +Don't stay??> in the faci<lities/.
Not 63954safe. Get out if y//alt:ou can. Outside.
Ple00801ase.
Not safe any//ent:where.
<JAC1895>

I stare at the screen. At first there is nothing. Shock, maybe. That tingle in my fingers I used to get in suspenseful movies when I was little. But then it starts to flow in like a stream, and then like a river, and finally an ocean wave. Rage. Utter, trembling, and burning rage. *His* fault? *He* did this to me? There's a part of me that already knew this. Or at least suspected. Didn't Varya say something about this earlier? Yes, I'm sure she did. So, yes. A part of me did know. The rest of me is coming to terms with it less than elegantly, because . . . I don't think I realized the extent of it. The sense of betrayal that never hit me before crashes in on me now.

Maybe I'm just an idiot, but I never even realized Joseph

liked me. Like beyond a slight weird attraction or the inkling of a feeling . . . we were just friends. I never felt anything for him or thought that he felt anything for me. But as I sit here, seething . . . I start to see the signs. He really did like me, didn't he? And he was trying to show it.

For about a millisecond I pity him, but anger has a way of killing the more human and logical emotions. Better still, it has a way of turning them sideways, backward, and upside down so that, instead of pitying him, I find him pathetic, conniving, and disgusting less than a second later. And then, after that passes, there's only anger. Only. Anger.

Because . . . Adam. *Adam.* He's dead. If Joseph caused all this . . . *did* he cause Adam's death? I can feel heat up my neck and am suddenly aware, once more, of Dekker, Jaxon, Germy, and Eli, who I now notice are looking at me. I look at each of them briefly, my eyes flitting quickly. I look back at the screen. *Here to make it right.* How can he possibly make any of this right? How pathetic does he have to be to think that he can just fix this? Nothing in my mind is true, and it's his fault. I'm stuffed full of trickery, lies, and chemicals that enforce those lies. I've been destroyed in the most cleverly evil manner. And he just told me it was his fault . . .

I swallow and close my eyes. I didn't realize I was walking away until my feet are pounding up the stairs. I run into Kelly's bedroom and slam the door. I grab my hair and turn around several times. My heart is pounding, my mind is swirling. I can't focus. I can't *think*! I'm so angry! I'm so . . .

I let out a groan-like sob and pull on my hair. Suddenly I'm inside my nightmare. The one I thought I'd defeated. Kelly's room fades to utter blackness and spins around me. I hit something and fall to my knees, gasping for breath, but I'm sinking. There's no voice other than my own. Screaming.

Just screaming. There are no words. There is nothing but the raw anger and terror that rips from me in the jagged scourge of my own scream. But then there's something else. I'm still screaming, but now there's blood. Coursing down over me.

I realize that I'm drowning in it. Drowning in blood. Not my own. *Adam's*. I can hear the sound of the gunshots over and over, getting louder and louder and surrounding me. I gasp and scream again. My throat is aching and my lungs are burning from the effort. I feel hands on my face and shoulders and scream harder, louder, more painfully.

"Devynn!"

I'm crying but screaming at the same time. It's the worst feeling in the world. I can't breathe—and I can't stop. And I can't see anything but the blood surrounding me.

"Devynn!" I can't . . . I can't breath. "Devynn, *please!*"

I can't stop. I can't see . . . hands on me . . . blood. Blood everywhere. I squeeze my eyes shut and clench my teeth. The sound of the gun. I scream, ruggedly through my teeth, and it tapers into a gravelly groan.

"Devynn, look at me."

I open my eyes and Kelly's room has reappeared. Lydia kneels before me. I'm on my hands and knees, trembling, panting, sweating. I stare at the carpet, whimpering as she rubs my shoulders.

"Hey . . . " She soothes, but I can't take it.

Everything just crashed in on me. I forgot everything. I forgot *Yeshua* . . . I forgot the peace. I feel the beginning of warmth and love filtering into my brittle form through Lydia's soft hands, and now that warmth robs me of breath. I gasp and start sobbing again, my elbows wavering. Lydia slides her arms under mine and pulls me against her. I transfer my grip to hold her close to me, sobbing heavily into her shoulder. The tension in my body shatters and trembles weakly in her embrace.

"Oh, My brokenhearted . . . "

TWELVE

Confirmation

That sticky sensation of a swollen face and salty eyes seems to be the only constant lately. That and the certainty that everything is sure to be unsure. I sit on Kelly's bed, calming . . . although calm is not a word I've used to describe myself in quite some time. I wipe my hands over my eyes.

"I'm . . . OK," I say to Lydia, even though I can't be sure that's entirely true. In fact, I'm pretty sure it's not.

"Are you sure?" she whispers, rubbing my shoulders.

I nod. "Yeah. Yeah, I think so." It's interesting how a white lie somehow feels OK in situations like this. As if Lydia knows I'm not OK, that I'm lying, but she'll let it slide because, at the moment, I'm stable. I sniff and stand up, feeling light-headed and wobbly on my feet.

Lydia stands up with me, eyes looking sympathetically into mine. I have told her everything—at least as much as I can—we have prayed together . . . and I am starting to think I really am OK. Stable. At least for now.

I get up and walk into Kelly's small attached master bathroom and splash some water across my face. *Joseph.* I sigh. I'm still angry and betrayed, but I have to acknowledge the courage it must have taken for him to reach out like that to us. The risk he's taking is immense. Perhaps even more than the risk we face ourselves. If he gets caught . . . I shudder to think what could happen to him. Even if there is part of me that could justify that he deserves it. That part is wrong.

I need to forgive him. It can't have been entirely his fault.

Unfortunately, only part of me believes that.

I start down the stairs, even though I'm sure I look like I've been crying, and I'm not sure I can take anyone asking me if I'm OK. Hopefully, they won't ask. Maybe they won't. My feet are heavy on the steps, though, so I try to brighten my face as I near the bottom.

I am greeted by several concerned looks, but no one asks me anything for now. I take a breath and walk over to where Eli and Germy are still absorbed; Dekker and Jaxon are standing nearby. Germy looks at me for a silent second or two and Eli takes a nervous glance, like looking at me might set me off again. I try to keep it light. "What did I miss?" My question seems ridiculous in light of everything I just went through—but I ask it anyway.

"Got another message," Germy calmly says.

My interest in all this returns. "Really? What does it say?"

"Well—" He points at the screen. The message reads Kelly's address and four words: *I covered you. Careful.*

The blood drains from my face. "He knows we're *here?*"

Germy nods. Exhales. "Yeah."

"But he covered for us," Dekker puts in. He shrugs as I turn to face him.

"Or so he says," Jaxon adds.

"Yes," Dekker says. "Whatever the story is . . . he *could* be an invaluable ally."

"Someone on the inside," Germy adds.

I try to nod, but I end up shaking my head. "I don't trust him," I say. *Did I really say that out loud?* I sigh after saying it, but quietly.

"I'm with her," Jaxon says. "I don't buy this."

Dekker nods. "I understand." He blinks. "I don't either."

Faintly, we can hear tiny Kuri beginning to cry. Upstairs I think. "I want to believe his story," I say, glancing back at the computer. "But he did crazy things before, and lied to my face about it over and over again." I hold up my hands. "I can't trust him. But that's just me. If we have to . . . " I drop my hands. Search for words, but I don't have any. "I don't trust him."

Dekker nods, thoughtfully, rubs his collarbone. And then: "Germy, can we communicate with him?"

"Working on that," Eli cuts in. "Yes, I think we can if I can . . . umm . . . "

"'Yes you think we can' is enough," Dekker says, then looks back at me. "If we can communicate with him . . . is there anything he could do that would satisfy you that we can trust him?"

I don't want to be that deciding factor. But I'm pretty sure I'm the only one here who knows him. I sigh. "Well, we have to verify that it's really him, first, right?"

"Probably a good idea," Eli throws in, not missing a beat with his typing or looking up from his work.

Dekker concedes this. "OK. Do you have something only he would know?"

I think. "I can probably come up with something." *I can, right?*

"OK." Dekker unfolds his arms. "So, once you know it's him . . . "

I swallow.

"What then?" Dekker continues. "You still won't trust him."

"Rightfully so," Jaxon says, a hint of a chuckle. Odd for anyone to be chuckling about any of this, but somehow it makes sense to do so at the same time.

Dekker looks at me. "Rightfully so," he repeats. "Is there anything he could do, or tell you, or give us that would make you trust him?" He pauses. "Anything that would tell us we can trust him?"

I bite a thumbnail. I hate that this has to rest on me. I try to think of something important. Something huge that he could do . . . nothing comes. I can't think of anything but betrayal. And the horrible thought that he could be playing us. I think of Adam. . . . I close my eyes and *stop* thinking about Adam. I have to, at least for now.

"Hang on," I say and head into the living room, where Varya seems to have woken up, because Kelly and Lydia are hovering over her. I walk over and kneel down, trying to smile. "Hey, Varya." She's the only other person who knows Joseph personally. I want to cut right to the chase. But she was also just shot, so I better start slow. "How are you feeling?"

She sighs. "Better." She winces. "But far from good." She adjusts slightly. She senses I want to ask her something. "What's up?"

"I just have a question." I bite my lip. "About Joseph Clere."

She furrows her brow. "Don't you know him?"

"Yeah, I do. But only socially."

"OK. Shoot," she says, actually looking, even in her condition, intrigued.

"What is something The Monarch or Petrov would never ever reveal to us? Something that Joseph has access to? Or can get to?"

Now Varya looks confused, but she is thinking about it anyway. "They were working on a new Rewrite program. They call it Genesis." She swallows. "They would never reveal anything about that." She looks at me pointedly. "Like . . . ever. Joseph probably only knows what he overhears about it." She furrows her brow once again, purses her lips. "But you said 'something he could get to.' And he could probably get to it." Then Varya shakes her head. "Wait. What is the point of this?"

I explain the whole situation, the fleece we're trying to devise.

"Ohh," she says. "OK. Yeah. Ask him to send you the formula for the new Rewrite serum. Do *not* specify Genesis." She makes quotations with her fingers on the word *Genesis*. "If he sends you anything not called Genesis or not heavily encrypted, then it isn't him. Or you can't trust him."

I nod. "OK. Thank you."

"No problem," she says sleepily. Then thinks a bit more. "But, really . . . it doesn't matter if it's him. If he sends you that file, then you can trust . . . whoever it is."

I nod, get up, and go back to Eli, Germy, and Dekker, explaining what we should do. "That is, if we can get a safe way to communicate with him."

Germy raises his eyebrows approvingly, Dekker nods, and Jaxon mutters something. Silence holds the room for a few long minutes, and then Eli stops typing and the silence thickens.

"Done," he says. I look at the blank screen and see the cursor blinking, waiting for us to type our message. To Joseph Clere, who I can no longer say is my friend.

Still . . . what do we say?

*****

JAC1895 confirm identity

Joseph sits up sharply from a spinning chair and almost falls out of it. He peers more closely at the screen, even though the words appear clearly. His heart rate spikes and he puts his fingers to the keys at once, but then withdraws them. To clearly state his name would be stupid. If someone decrypted the message, it would be a fatal mistake to have identified himself. He bites the inside of his cheek and types.

Clarify.
JAC1895 confirm identity. Send latest serum/formula.

Joseph's heart sinks as he reads the words. *Send them the formula for the new serum? He* doesn't even have access to that. Not the new serum, anyway . . . Do they really want the new serum? He could send them the old formula. It would be much easier to get to. Sweat breaks out on Joseph's forehead as he ponders what they're asking of him. He puts his face in his hands. Breathes out sharply through his fingers, then takes a deep breath. And types.

Very dangerous. New program is called Genesis. Heavy encryption.

He holds his breath as he waits for a reply, prays they won't ask him to retrieve it for them. But even as he waits, he prepares to do what The Monarch has deemed impossible, and that is to steal information about the Genesis Program.

Send encrypted file/serum//formula.

Joseph rubs his temple and sighs heavily. And once again begins his reply . . .

Retrieving file/Genesis Serum

*****

We wait breathlessly. More breathless than I think I've ever been. In fact, I think I forgot to breathe for about a minute. I think everyone else did too.

Once we get down to it, it's not about the serum. We don't specifically need the formula of the substance that caused all this. It's about *proof.* And I'm now thinking we're gonna get it. I'm beginning to think that it really is Joseph. And if it is, my emotions aside, we have someone three feet from the President on our side. The tingle in my fingers reappears, and I bite a fingernail to keep it at bay.

* * * * *

We haven't received a reply in almost half an hour, and no one has moved. In fact, we've barely shifted. Sha, Benjamin, and Jaxon now stand with us, just as still and also anticipating. We all gasp at exactly the same instant when a message appears.

Confirm: send??

I think Eli almost fell out of his chair. And, typing now, it looks like he's still trying *not* to.

Confirm.

We wait again, but this time only for about five minutes . . . and the computer basically explodes. Line upon line of complicated sequences. I realize that I know exactly what is filling out before my eyes! I get it! It's . . .

Complete and utter gibberish.

I don't understand a single letter, number, or symbol that flies across the screen. But the more that comes through the more excited Germy, Eli, and Sha seem to get. For once, I don't feel completely alone, as Dekker and Jaxon seem a little behind themselves. But the main comfort is Benjamin, who looks as deeply bewildered and confused as I am. Once the numbers stop coming in, Germy and Sha both seem to take deep breaths.

"Whoa," Sha says as Eli scrolls up and down the information

we've received.

"Wow," Germy says. "I think that's the craziest encryption I've ever seen."

"We don't need to decrypt the whole thing," Dekker says, taking a step forward. "We just need to make sure it's the Genesis file, and not something outdated."

"Mmm," Eli mutters. "I'm just, uh . . . not even sure I can do that."

"Yeah, you can," Sha scolds. "Look right there." She points. "Bam!"

"Nice!" Germy says, pulling up a chair.

"All right. Umm . . . hang on," Eli says, exiting the file and returning to the conversation window to type a one-word message.

Received.

"Here we go," Sha says, and Eli begins to type, zoning out of everything but whatever is directly in front of his face or at the tips of his fingers.

The small group that had congregated slowly dissolves until Germy, Sha, and Eli are the only ones watching what is happening with the thick encryption. I sit in front of the television, trying—but failing—to forget everything that is happening at the moment. To just chill. But . . . emphasis on *failing*. Dekker and Jaxon are behind me in the living room, devising more plans.

"If he really wants to help us, then we should take full advantage of that. And fast," Jaxon says. "We don't want him to have a change of heart. We need a way out of here."

For a long moment, Dekker doesn't reply. Then he does. "They're taking everyone out of here," he says matter-of-factly, referring to evacuations we are all but sure are going to happen.

"Yeah, but we can't go with them. They'd flag us," Jaxon says.

"Right," Dekker says. "But they can't all just recognize us by face. Our files show us to be Resistant. Half of them probably won't even recognize us without those files in front of them."

"OK," Jaxon says.

"So . . . if we can get Joseph to edit our files and our digital identities—somehow—we could potentially slip in with the evacuations when they begin."

Jaxon thinks about it. "Yeah, potentially. But . . . " His voice lowers below what I can hear.

I sigh. Everyone's restless. Bailey and Allen sit on the floor. Bailey looks asleep on his lap, but he rubs her hair and shoulders in a manner that seems forcibly smooth. Then he stops and bounces his knee. Sarah and Emma are both asleep, leaning on each other on the couch beside me. Laura stands off to the side, rubbing her mouth, not looking at the television at all. I don't even know what it's playing, and I don't care enough to check. Benjamin leans on the couch behind me. Serena is around, I'm sure, but I don't see her. I haven't seen much of her, actually. She probably needs space to breathe.

I think Lydia and Zachary are upstairs because I haven't seen either of them in a while. But when I turn, I see they're both in the living room with Varya. Paige is upstairs for sure. I can hear them moving around, and the occasional baby sounds from Kuri. Moses, who I realize is very dear to me in some part of my heart, is snoring softly in a big armchair, covered with a blanket that I imagine Lydia has draped over him.

I can't believe there are so few of us. And now with Myah, Christopher, and Adam gone, not to mention Varya wounded, there are less. We gained Jaxon and Paige, their baby, and Kelly—I guess, maybe—but we're still so shorthanded. I can't even fathom that we've made it this far. That we who remain are still alive.

And Chloe! In the moment of respite and thinking of

people other than myself or those immediately around me, I realize I've forgotten her. But now that I remember, a dozen thoughts swarm my mind in an instant. I don't know how we're going to get her out. Where is she, even? I hope she's OK. I pray she's OK. I'm going to have to tell her about Adam. I swallow that back for now. No reason to think about that yet.

I exhale, close my eyes, and lean my head back. *Lord, please give me peace for tonight.*

Within five minutes, I am asleep.

THIRTEEN

Assessment

The funny thing is I never used to sleep on couches. I *couldn't* fall asleep. But that has changed completely. In fact, I think I have gotten some of my most recent best nights' sleeps on couches. Guess I can sleep wherever now. Small blessings.

All that goes through my mind before my eyes even open, and when they do, I heave a still-tired sigh. Emma is still asleep beside me, and when I get up, I make sure not to wake her. I hear the sound of a shower running, and it is the most relaxing thing I've heard in a while. It's not like I haven't heard a shower running these past weeks; I just haven't been able to relax and appreciate the sound of running water. Everyone here could use a shower. But we'll just have to deal with some slightly sweaty aromas for now. Everyone's nerves are being stretched to the absolute limit.

Still sleepy, I scratch my head as I enter the main room and see everyone kind of hanging around, not sure what to do. Eli looks like he just woke up from sleeping on the keyboard all night, and his face has weird sleep lines on it. His hair is standing almost completely on end. He sniffs and begins to sleepily scrutinize the computer.

Sha looks frazzled, Germy looks groggy, and I think Benjamin is literally asleep where he's standing. Lydia, Kelly, and Laura are in the kitchen, I think, and I see a blonde head that can only be Serena's. I peer into the living room and see Dekker sitting on the couch opposite Varya. He's probably the most alert person I've seen yet, and *he* looks like he could sleep for a week. He looks at Varya intently. Thoughtfully.

I look at her. She looks horrible. She's asleep, but her skin appears cadaverous. She doesn't move at all, other than her breathing. Beyond that, she could be dead. I glance at Dekker, uncertainly. His eyes flick to mine. He clenches his jaw as he looks back in her direction. Then he sighs and brings his hand over his eyes, massaging his forehead.

"Did you sleep?" I turn to see Serena standing behind me, looking pointedly at Dekker. I recall how, at Rendezvous Point, he only slept a few hours before we assaulted the Capitol. I also recall how mothering Serena was.

He shrugs without looking at her. "A little."

She raises an eyebrow at him, but doesn't push for more. There's a few seconds of weary silence, and I feel like I could probably fall asleep again.

"What if it's not him?" Jaxon says, entering the living room from the kitchen, Paige at his side.

"I don't know, Jaxon. We'll know soon enough," Dekker says.

"Let him be," Paige says, gently, to Jaxon. Jaxon heeds his wife's admonition.

I figure I should contribute something, as well as alleviate some of the tension developing between Jaxon and Dekker. But I can't. All I can do is add more. "We have another issue," I say. I really don't want to bring it up, but somebody has to. "What are we going to do about Chloe?"

"Who's Chloe?" Jaxon asks.

"An FC. She's alive in the Capitol," Dekker says, like he'd

forgotten about her, and reminding him was probably like adding a ton of bricks to the load on his shoulders.

"Why are we just now thinking of this?" Jaxon asks. More tension and responsibility Dekker's way, courtesy of Jaxon. And I guess from me as well.

"She was comatose. No one knew she was alive except us," Benjamin puts in.

"But we probably don't have long before that wears off," Dekker says. "We're gonna have to figure out how to get her before we get out of here."

"Get out of here?" It's Sha, speaking up from the opposite side of the room. "Do you have a plan?"

Dekker sighs. "Not quite. Just the beginning of one."

Eli makes a sharp yelp from the other room; Serena and I jump. Dekker is on his feet in about a tenth of a second.

"I got it!" Eli yells.

We flock around the computer. Everyone who heard him—and this includes Serena, Sha, Benjamin, Dekker, Paige, Jaxon, Germy, who was already there next to him, the three other girls in the kitchen, and me—practically runs over to see the screen. I can barely see the monitor; everyone is pressing for a glimpse. I see the full screen for about a second and can make out a single clear word: *Genesis*.

I gasp, and it spreads through the room. We have it. The *proof*. The decrypted file. We actually have it. Now we know we have an ally we can trust.

Maybe now we have a chance.

*****

"All right. We'll start from the top," Petrov says. "What's your name?"

"Ryan Watson." He answers without hesitation.

"What is your age?"

"Twenty-two."

"What happened that put you in ICU?"

"My car was attacked by a mob in Russia." Ryan doesn't blink or break eye contact.

"Who were you driving?"

"Eliza Carver and Caleb Solomon." He scratches his head. Relaxes his posture. Like he's bored.

Petrov smiles. "Why were you with them?"

"I was their security detail."

"What happened?" Petrov asks, lowering his tone.

Ryan takes a breath. "I was shot twice. Caleb suffered a head injury and Eliza was beaten severely." He swallows. Clenches his jaw. "Caleb is now dead."

Petrov nods solemnly. "That's right."

Ryan sets his teeth and looks away.

Petrov lets a minute go by in silence. "You're doing really well. Your memory seems to be improving, right?"

Ryan nods and takes a breath, looks over to meet Petrov's eyes. "Yeah. I don't want to stop, it's just . . . " He lets out a puff of air through his nose. "I don't know. This ticks me off."

"I know. I'm sorry. We'll move on." Petrov adjusts in his chair. "OK, what is the current situation?"

Ryan sits up straighter. "Well, the San Francisco Veil has been compromised. By acts of the Resistant, led by the radical, Dekker Myrus."

The disdain that laces the words *Resistant, radical,* and *Dekker Myrus* is one of the most satisfying things Petrov has ever heard.

"As a result, the whole city is compromised," Ryan continues. He swallows. "The citizens are under Lockdown, so they're probably all still in the dark about what happened. Hopefully, they stay that way."

"And if they don't?"

Ryan narrows his eyes, thinks hard. "Well then, we'll

Rewrite them. Or infect them"—he puts *infect* in air quotes—"and send them to Russia."

"Correct." Petrov shoots him a thumbs-up. "And why?"

"To ensure peace and order." Ryan answers automatically, a little too much so, and Petrov starts to go off the book.

"What gives us the right to do that?" he asks, tilting his head to one side.

Ryan blinks. Pauses. Then answers as if it is the most natural thing in the world. "Because the people can't be trusted to think for themselves. And chaos would result." He shrugs. "We've created the perfect utopia. They just can't see it that way." He folds his arms casually. "Rewriting isn't a bad thing. It ensures everyone's happiness. The ends justify the means a hundred times over."

Petrov nods—just like a therapist, he thinks. "So you wouldn't care if *you* were to be Rewritten?"

Ryan chuckles. "Well, I think I'd care, but . . . I mean, if it were for the greater good then . . . " He inhales and exhales. "Then, no. No, I wouldn't care."

"Hmm," Petrov says. "Why not?"

"Because the new memories I'd get would be better than the ones I'd lost." He shrugs. "People who have been Rewritten are some of the happiest people in this whole society."

Petrov chuckles, actually chuckles. "They're the lucky ones."

Ryan scoffs with a smile. "I know, right? Ignorance is bliss."

"Exactly." Petrov sighs contentedly. He slaps his hand on the list of questions. "All right! Next question." He clears his throat as Ryan straightens. "Here's a tough one. List the first names of the living Resistant."

"Ooh . . . " Ryan says and looks up. He bites his lip as he thinks. Then he laughs lightly. "You're right. That is a tough one. Umm . . . "

Petrov waits expectantly.

Ryan holds up his hands to start counting. "Just first names, right?"

"Yup."

"All right. There's Dekker Myrus"—the full, hated name just rolls off his tongue—"Gerald, Serena . . . Emma, Sarah, Laura, Lydia, Devynn . . . "

Petrov holds his breath as Ryan says her name, but he doesn't pause or show any change of expression.

" . . . Zachary, Moses, Benjamin, Allen, Bailey, Jaxon and Paige and their kid, Kuri . . . and uh . . . " His eyes flit nervously. "Varya Petrov. Whom we assume is still alive."

Petrov purses his lips, then relaxes. "That's all of them. Good job." He swallows back the confusing array of emotions that surrounds that last name. *Is my sister alive? Is she working with them?* He doesn't know. He might never know. "All right, who all have they lost?"

"Chloe Allison, Adam Taurine, Christopher something-or-other, and a girl named Myah. Possibly Varya. We don't know for sure." He leans back casually.

Petrov's heart rate is up a bit, but hearing Ryan bounce over Taurine's name so easily is settling. "All right." He looks at Ryan sideways. "How are you feeling?"

"Good," Ryan says with a bright nod. "Great, actually."

"Good! I'm glad. Last question."

"Shoot."

"What do we do with the Resistant?"

"Rewrite them." No hesitation at all in Ryan's response.

"And if they won't be Rewritten?"

He blinks. "Then we kill them."

* * * * *

"His progress is . . . it's groundbreaking, sir. We've never tracked anything so . . . monumental. Unprecedented. In training he's physically excelling, and mentally—I can't begin to tell you how well the serum is taking. This is truly incredible, sir."

Once again, the cursor is moving and letters are flying across the screen.

And 003?

Petrov sighs. "She's doing fine. Recovering. We started her on the serum with a higher dose, and we'll start the therapy soon, but I think the biggest asset here is Ryan. He could be a huge success. I want to keep him out of the San Francisco area, though, to avoid any triggers."

Genesis was designed to withstand such triggers. Do you suspect a weakness in the formula?

"Uh . . . no, sir. I just think we should play it safe." Petrov shifts his weight uneasily.

I disagree.

Petrov swallows.

San Francisco is compromised. Expand your horizons. Push the serum. Send him back.

Petrov blinks several times. "But . . . sir, if we fail—"

You have ALREADY failed.

Petrov doesn't reply.

This is the crucible. Send him back. If the serum cannot withstand the triggers, then we terminate him, and the San Francisco Trial as well.

"Sir! The whole trial?" Petrov takes several steps toward the screen on which the cursor blinks. The silence in the room seems to thicken when no reply is typed for nearly a minute. Petrov's face flushes heat.

"Yes, sir," he says, frustration and disappointment thickening his voice.

Is the contingency in place?

"Yes, sir." He drops his head into his hand. "His last surgery secured the implant."

Good. So should the contingency hold, then perhaps your trial may be spared. If not, we terminate. Are we clear?

Petrov clenches his jaw tightly, hands planted firmly on his hips.

The previous message clears.

Are we clear, Dmitri?

Petrov tastes metal. This risk is completely unnecessary. It's like The Monarch is setting him up to fail. Yes, the serum is strong, and yes, there is the contingency, but . . . to throw Ryan back into an environment that is practically designed to remind him of everything they want him to forget, is . . . reckless. Ridiculous.

Are we clear?

Petrov exhales sharply. "Yes, sir."

The screen goes black.

FOURTEEN

A Decision

I'm one of the first people awake in the morning, and I head down to the living room. It feels like everything—and nothing—has happened at the same time for the past day and a half. Or however long. Honestly, I've lost track. Like, despite everything, we've accomplished nothing. It's a frustrating feeling, and I know it's not an accurate one. The dome is shut down. The trio is decrypting the Genesis File. We've moved from the facility into the city . . . Varya's still alive . . . but Chloe still needs rescuing. And yet nothing seems to have happened. I feel the same inside as I did seconds after Adam died. I don't feel healed, or stronger, or even weaker. I don't really feel anything.

Laura sits on the floor by Varya, chatting. I sit on the love seat directly opposite the two of them, thus inviting myself into their conversation.

Varya nods in the direction of the couch. I turn my head and see Dekker, asleep, head in his hand.

I stick out my lip. "Poor guy," I whisper. "How long has he been out?"

Laura shakes her head. "I dunno. Half an hour at least."

Varya looks at me. "How are you?" she asks, quietly.

I chuckle. "I'm hanging in there. How are you?"

Now she gives a light laugh. "Better, I think. I mean, for having been target practice, I guess I'm pretty good."

Laura smirks. Then turns to me, her bright, strong eyes softened. "I'm so sorry. About everything." She sighs.

I avert my gaze, not sure if I can hold hers. "Me too." I swallow. Tears. I sigh and look up, blinking them back. Then I laugh in that sad way that means I'm trying not to cry. "But it's gonna be OK." I look at her. "We trust in Him."

She nods, sympathetically. "Because He is good."

I nod and wipe my eyes.

Varya is looking at me, then she looks at Laura and at me again. "You guys have so much faith."

Neither of us answer. Laura nods slightly.

"I know everything about what you believe. . . . And honestly I probably believe it too." Her voice trails off; she shakes her head. "But you guys trust your lives to something you can't see." Her eyes flit from me to Laura a few times. "I can't fathom it." She laughs, a type of small, sad laugh. "But I'm also kinda jealous of it." She shifts farther down into the couch.

I look at Laura and she at me; we hold each other's gaze. How much faith do I have, really? How much does she have? We can say all day long that we trust Him . . . but how much *do* we? How much do we just rely on Him instead of worrying our heads off? How often do we just lean on Him and rest in peace? I look down, lost in thought.

"Faith is a funny thing," Laura says, folding her arms. "I don't think any of us has enough faith. I don't think we ever will. We always need more, no matter how much or how little we have."

Varya looks confused about this, but holds her peace.

"Lydia," Laura says with a smile, "for example. She's like . . . the most trusting and faithful person I know."

Varya and I both smile widely. We agree.

"But she needs more faith just as much as I do. Just as much as you do," Laura says, looking to me. Then she looks to Varya. "And just as much as you do."

Varya shrugs. "I guess." She closes her eyes. Then opens them, her face serious. "Trust isn't my forte, though."

Yeah. I remember that Petrov is her brother. *Ouch.*

"Mine either," Laura puts in.

I shake my head, agreeing with both. "I don't think trust is any of our fortes," I say, leaning back on the couch. "I mean . . . just look at where we are."

After a second both of them laugh—Varya carefully so.

"Our lives are all lies," she finally says, softly.

Everyone is quiet after that.

"We can't trust anything we know," I continue. "Except what we read in the Bible. And what God reveals to us." I swallow. "That is the only thing that's real. The *only* thing." Silence holds the three of us for about a minute. Then we see Dekker shift on the couch, and we turn to see him waking.

"Morning," Varya says, good-naturedly.

He blinks a few times, then sighs. "Was I asleep?"

Laura replies. "Like a rock."

Dekker drags a hand through his hair, then stands up. I almost want to tell him to go back to sleep, but he's already walking into the dining room to join the trio, which is frowning collectively at the computer screen.

Serena enters the living room, passing Dekker. She looks at us, then jabs a thumb back in Dekker's direction. "Wasn't he just asleep?"

I nod. "He just woke up."

She rolls her eyes. "He won't sleep. He's impossible." She marches after him, muttering grumpily.

Varya follows her out with her eyes, snickering to herself. Then she sighs. "I'm so done laying here."

"You cannot get up yet," Laura says sternly. "No way. You

could have internal injuries. You gotta rest."

Varya glares playfully. "Fine." Then she settles in and closes her eyes. "Go see what they're talking about. I'm sleeping."

Laura chuckles. "G'night."

I smile and get up. I wander into the kitchen. It's like stepping into another atmosphere. From drowsiness to tension. There's a discussion brewing, I can tell. The air is full of this horrible, maddening sense of nothing to do but worry about everything we've left behind and everything that lies ahead. It has a hold on everyone. I can read it behind their eyes, hear it in their voices, see it in their movements. The stress has heightened to an entirely new level. Everyone seems ready to snap.

"We need to get to work on this," Jaxon says. "We need clean files so we won't set off alarms if we try to leave."

"OK, but there's more to that than it seems," Germy says. "We can't just hit delete and make up something new. Not to mention the facial recognition software that's all over the place here."

"I understand," Jaxon says. "I'm not trying to say we need it done right now, but we don't want to waste our time."

"Jaxon's right," Dekker says. "We need to start on that if it's going to take a while."

"Umm . . . " Eli starts, and all eyes in the room travel to him. "I don't think we can pull this off. Not from here. Not with what we have." He gestures to Kelly's laptop. "This thing just isn't enough."

"We have Joseph," Jaxon says.

"And here I was thinking you didn't trust him," Allen says, the accusation pretty obvious.

Jaxon looks at him. "I don't. But we need his help, and I don't see any other solutions." He holds Allen's eyes for another tense second. He looks away. "We need to leave."

"We need to get Chloe," Zachary says.

Everyone mutters agreement.

"Yes," Jaxon says, but I can see in his eyes he'd rather gloss over that issue. "We do need to get her, but if we get her and we have no plan on how we're going to get out of here, then it's useless. There's no point."

"We don't even know if she's still there," Benjamin says softly, pointing out what no one else wants to. There's a breath of silence. "I hope she is . . . but I'm not going to pretend there's no possibility she isn't. We should take that into account. That's all I'm saying."

"He has a point," Jaxon says. "If we go and get her, we risk being seen by someone, and she might not even be there."

No one says anything. There are no solutions. We need about fifty things done at once, and we can't accomplish any of them. As if in answer to the stifling silence, something outside groans and screeches loudly. Eyes widen, and after the sound stops, the silence is thicker. I can hear my heart pounding for several seconds before the boom sounds. Another section of the Veil has fallen. We look around, our breath taken. What must have been at least a minute transpires without a whisper, and then Dekker walks to the Decontamination area at the front of the house. He shoves the plastic door aside and tries to look through the tiny, almost opaque window in the front door.

I realize that, without noticing, I and most of the group that congregated in the dining room has followed him there. We can't see anything. The window is useless, but the sound was close. It had to have been.

Dekker pushes back to the dining room as we each take a turn trying to get our faces to the glass and see through; we don't want to risk opening the door again. But something about that chunk of the Veil falling brings two things: hope and utter terror. Hope because maybe it will all come down. Maybe we'll be free. And terror because, at any second, one of those falling pieces could crash and kill us. And also terror because we have to leave this home, and find Chloe, risking all of that, and still we could get killed. By falling debris.

I sigh and go back to the living room, feeling more useless and sheeplike than ever.

Dekker studies the surface of the table as if it holds all the answers to our conundrums. Jaxon doesn't say anything; no one else does either. We all just wait for Dekker to speak next, and I can't imagine the stress that puts on him. He rubs his eyebrow with the heel of his hand and looks up at all of us. "We need a decision."

I swallow and look around uncertainly.

"What do you guys want do?" he asks, simply.

"Get Chloe," Benjamin says.

"We could also get crushed!" Bailey puts in.

"So could she," Dekker adds.

"We're just as likely to be crushed here as anywhere else," Laura says flatly.

I don't know what to say to that. I suppose she's right, but we have to be safer here than out in the open, right? She's not suggesting that the house doesn't offer any protection, just stating a fact in a rather pessimistic way.

The thought in the room is so thick I swear I could slice it with a knife. Finally, Dekker speaks. "Opening the door before set something off. Joseph covered us, but we can't be sure he can do it again. And we would need him to do it twice more at least."

"We could always ask him," Sha says.

"We could," Dekker says, nodding more to himself than to her. "But we are not sure Chloe is still in the Capitol. And if she's not, by involving Joseph in this, we could give her away. If she's alive." He rubs an eyebrow. He just sounds tired.

"Hey!" We all turn toward the living room. "Can you guys kinda migrate over here or something?" Varya says. "I'm awake."

Someone chuckles, and I can't help a little smile as well as we make our way to the living room. We all settle in uneasily. Several who sit bounce their knees, but most remain standing.

Varya looks up at us all. "Chloe is probably waking up any time now. If she's not in the Capitol, and is with my brother in Russia . . . " She shrugs. "There's nothing we can do for her." She pauses briefly. "But if she wakes up in the Capitol, she could set off a dozen alarms."

"She's smart, though. She might stay still," Bailey says.

"If she thinks of it," Varya says. "She'll probably be very disoriented for at least a day after the meds wear off enough for her to be conscious. We should get her, but we have no way of knowing if she's even there, or if the Capitol is being guarded." She sighs. "I'd ask Joseph."

Murmurs of disapproval spread through the room.

"And risk giving up that Chloe is alive?" I'm not sure who said it, but they give voice to the thought we all have, and what Dekker had said a minute before.

"What choice do we have?" Varya asks, effectively silencing the disagreement. "If we stay here, we could die. And so could she." She looks around the room slowly. "If we leave here, we could die, and so could she—but she'd be with us. One problem at a time." She looks at Dekker. "I know we need to get out of here, but unless we want to leave her and then come back . . . " Her voice trails off; she sighs. "I say we get her as soon as we can. We're running out of time. The Veil isn't going to settle. Pieces are going to keep falling." No one has anything to say to refute that. "Someone needs to go get her, and Germy, Eli, and Sha can try to get Joseph on board and work out how we get out of here." She looks at Jaxon. "If we wait to get Chloe, she could wake up and get herself caught. And the longer we wait the more unstable the Veil gets. And the more pieces are going to fall."

Jaxon nods.

All eyes once again rest on Dekker. He looks up slowly.

"I agree with Varya." He crosses his arms and looks at her. "Realistically, when is she going to wake up?"

Varya thinks for a second. "Based on the dose . . . she could already be awake. If she's still alive."

"If she's still *alive*?" Benjamin cuts in, alarmed.

"Yeah. If," Varya says. "They put her in a freezer, which is fine since the drug will preserve her completely for about two days. We're past that mark." She thinks. "But because the dome shut down, the freezer probably isn't working."

Eli nods his head. "No, there shouldn't be any power in the Capitol at all."

"Right," Varya says, using lots of energy to think deeply about this problem. "So, even though the full strength was gone after two days, the temperature isn't an issue. Veriline is meant for low temperatures. She's fine in that regard for probably an extra two, maybe three days. But it had to have been at least that long while the freezer was still on." She shifts. "But now that it's off, it's been—what?—three or four days or something?"

"Almost four," Dekker says.

I can't believe it's been *only* four days and yet *already* four. Wow.

"Yeah," Varya says. "She should be awake." She nods. "If she's not already, she will be in . . . " She shrugs. "Less than a day. Hours, probably."

"So we have to get her. Pretty much now," Jaxon says, scratching his chin.

Varya nods. Looks at Dekker. "Yeah. Pretty much. We can't wait. If she's still there, and waking up, then she's still alive. I risked a lot to keep her that way, so . . . yeah. We gotta get her." Jaxon nods.

"Pretty much now," Dekker says, repeating Jaxon, his eyes moving from Jaxon to Varya.

Varya sighs. Nods. "We better try to talk to Joseph."

FIFTEEN

Chloe

They'd asked him so many questions that were so random, his curiosity was piqued. First they'd said they needed their files cleaned. That was a crazy task, and they hadn't even let him wrap his brain around that. They asked whether anyone was guarding the Capitol. He'd answered honestly: yes. They'd asked how many. He'd checked and told them there were only four officials.

Then they asked about internal motion detectors, and if any had been tripped. He'd told them he didn't see any alarms triggered. He'd tried to ask why they needed to know, but they just shut him down. The last thing they said was that they planned to open the door within the hour and needed him to make sure the alarm didn't trigger.

So Joseph is waiting. He'd disabled the alarm nearly twenty minutes ago and given them the go-ahead. But they haven't opened the door yet from what he can tell. He sits, uneasily, checking over his shoulder at least every five minutes. He looks and sees no one.

He gives his attention to the screen, watching the front door of Kelly's house, making sure the alarm doesn't automatically reengage.

"Joseph!"

He startles. Spins in his chair. Petrov stands before him, smiling. "Mister President!" His heart is racing, his head feels light. His tongue is leaden.

"What are you up to?"

"Uhh . . . nothing. Just, um . . . " He turns, moving the cursor quickly. "I was just checking security cameras." He turns back to Petrov. "You know, just checking on some . . . some friends and family over there."

Petrov looks at him, pity, not skepticism, filling his eyes. Then it fades. "Have you seen anything I should know about?"

Joseph shakes his head. "No. I am on the lookout, though."

"Good. I'm glad somebody is." He chuckles and draws up a chair, facing the screen and Joseph, who faces away from the screen. "I'm sending Ryan there now."

Joseph's blood cools until it's frigid. "What? Why? It's been less than a week since—"

"No, he's completely healed. It's amazing."

That is amazing. "Whoa," Joseph says, trying to sound interested, but internally screaming. "Uh . . . why would you risk sending him back? There's probably a lot of triggers there, right?"

Petrov shakes his head. "It was suggested that he should be treated as the first test subject and should face every challenge as it arises." He shrugs. "He passed the final physical and mental exam last night, and I have something I need him to check."

Joseph blinks. "What is that?"

"Chloe Allison."

Joseph swallows. Something clicks into place in his mind, but he can't tell what it is.

"It was . . . suggested that I make sure she is dead." He taps his fingers anxiously on the chair. "We'll see how he reacts to the stimuli, and if he withstands everything, then . . . " He lets the sentence trail off.

Joseph grits his teeth, fights the urge to turn around, to make sure the alarm is still disengaged, to see if they've left already. And then it hits him. Like a freight train. The open door. The Capitol . . . it's all about Chloe. They're going for her body. Either that or . . . she is somehow alive, like The Monarch seems to think. Dread seeps through Joseph. And now Petrov is sending Ryan to the Capitol.

"Well, I've got things to do." Petrov slaps his hands together and stands. "Keep me posted."

Joseph smiles and nods, both actions feeling forced and terrified. He sits still for several seconds, until Petrov's footsteps disappear. Then he spins in the chair. And sees that the alarm is still disengaged. But the door has already opened—and shut again.

*****

URGENT! STOP! Do not go to the Capitol.

I squint at the message. "Why not?" I ask aloud. Dekker, Jaxon, Allen, and Benjamin left to go and get Chloe about five minutes ago! Joseph had just told us we were covered and that the group could go.

Eli frowns at the screen. Types.

Reason?

Change of circumstance. Dangerous person en route.

A chill runs up my spine. They could be almost a mile from here by now. Dekker said they'd be running. But we can't stop them, can we? They *have* to get Chloe. If she wakes up with whoever this person is, then she could get herself killed. "What do we do?" I put voice to the question ringing in my head.

Eli is typing.

Four people en route already. Retrieving ITEM XYZ.

Terminate.

ITEM XYZ Perishable. Invaluable.
Cannot terminate. Suggest options.

Terminate. Confirm: ITEM XYZ is Chloe Allison.

The breath is sucked from the room. "Don't answer that!" someone over my shoulder says.

Cannot confirm. Cannot terminate. Suggest options.

ITEM XYZ and the four people you sent could die. Not worth it. Terminate.

Everyone breathes hard. "We have to stop them," I say, and before I am thinking at all, I'm rushing for the door.

Germy grabs me and pulls me back. "What are you thinking?" he says. "You can't go."

"Why not? I know the city," I insist, pulling my arm away. I'm briefly aware of how bratty I sound, but I only care about that for a second. "They're all gonna get killed. Someone has to stop them!"

He blinks. Grabs a sweater and throws it over his head. "I'll go too."

"No!" I say. "You can't go. You're the only one besides Eli and Sha who knows the technology stuff you do. I *know* this city. I'll be fine." I grab Kelly's jacket from the rack and put it on.

Germy frowns, but knows I'm right. At least right-*ish*. So he figures that's not good enough. "I'm going," he insists.

I give up. "OK."

Germy spins around, speaks to Eli. "Tell him to cover the door."

Eli, very simply, is slow to catch on. He looks at us like we just proposed waking the dead—or something equally ridiculous. "You guys are leaving?"

"Yes," Germy says with finality. "Tell Joseph to cover the door."

About forty-five seconds later, Eli tells us it's covered. We open the door, fly out of it, and close it behind us as soon as possible. The realization that now I have to get Germy from here, probably all the way to the Capitol, in the dark without getting seen sinks in like the cold that seeps directly into my skin. I gasp. I can't believe how freezing it is. The dome isn't as dark as I remember it, and looking toward where the light is coming from, I can see that the original hole has widened to about twice its initial size. But it's even colder than I remember it after it first shut down. It's *bitter* out here.

Germy lets out a puff of air. "That's cold." He jams his hands in his pockets and starts walking. "Come on. We have to hurry. They're probably at least halfway there."

He sets out at a steady jog and heads straight across the street into an alley opposite Kelly's door. I keep going until I'm right next to him and match his pace. It's freezing! My ears and nose already feel numb, and even my eyeballs seem colder than usual. It isn't long before my whole face is painfully cold, and I can't feel my fingers at all.

We continue on for several streets, then round a corner slowly.

My stomach jumps when I see two men standing at the end

of the adjacent street. I gasp and step to the rear, backing into Germy. I shake my head. "Go around!" I mouth and push past him in the other direction. It's a detour, but we're almost there.

Finally, the Capitol looms in our view. We get as close as we can, but I can't see any of the four men who should be near this spot, guarding.

"Do you see anyone?" I whisper hoarsely.

"No," Germy replies, just as hoarse. "They could be inside already."

"Isn't there an access to the Underground Transportation System in there?" It was indicated on the maps we drew of the Capitol before we stormed it. That's a few days ago now, I guess. Feels like years ago. And yet it's all still as vivid as yesterday.

"Yeah, there is." Germy looks at me.

"Which means, if they're in there . . . " I swallow back the thought.

"They could be trapped. Cut off. We don't know." Germy rubs his hands together furiously and breathes on them.

"What do we do?" I ask, suddenly feeling useless, an all too common feeling of late.

"Well . . . " He thinks, cranes his head around the corner. "I don't see anyone there." He looks at me. "I think we can make it."

My fingers are tingling and my head buzzing. "I don't know. Is that a good idea?"

"We gotta try, right?" Germy says. He starts walking out in the open, slowly, toward the Capitol building.

I bite my tongue to keep from trying to stop him, and instead follow him, straining my eyes to see everything around me. The lighting is just enough to set my teeth on edge because any shape I see could be a person. And any shape I have to look at twice seems to become one, no matter what it actually is.

My heart is beating faster than I ever knew it could; I can feel the adrenaline coursing through me. It's like every inch of me is tingling. Or covered in a thousand ants. Everything I pass feels like a face turning to look at me, and every beat of my heart could be footsteps racing toward me.

When we reach the Capitol building, I don't think I've blinked in something like five minutes.

Germy turns to face me. "You OK?" he mouths.

I nod frantically, completely revealing my answer to be a lie—and telling him that I'm freaking out.

Still, he nods calmly. "Ready?"

I nod in return. He moves to the heavy oak door and begins to swing it open. He opens it just enough to begin to peer in. "I don't see anyone," he says over his shoulder in my direction.

I swallow.

He inches the heavy door open a little more. "Still nothing." He steps in slowly.

My heart pounds so loudly I can't hear anything else, but I step in after him, acutely aware of my breath shivering with each pull of my lungs against the icy air. He's a few steps ahead of me, and I close the distance a bit. I don't want to fall behind, and I can barely see.

Of course, it's at this moment that my mind recollects every scary movie and every jump scare I've ever been frightened by, and my eyes widen, trying to see more—but all I see is less. My heart pounds even louder, and I jerk my head around to check the side I'd been ignoring. There's nothing there, of course, but terror isn't something easily shaken. I swallow and work to keep up with Germy.

"Varya said she'd be downstairs, right?"

I jump at the sound of his voice. I swallow and nod. "Yeah."

He sighs. "That'd put it right next to the access to the UTS."

"Yeah." My tongue is dry in my mouth. I feel coiled, like a spring. We reach the staircase a few painstaking seconds later. I'm shivering, but I'm not sure if it's because of the cold or the fear. Probably both. The entire building is dark. No lights shine from anywhere except what dreary light filters in through opaque windows. I guess whatever virus Eli and Sha developed really packed a wallop.

Germy starts down the stairs and my heart stops. "Germy, wait."

He turns and looks at me. I can barely breathe. "Are you sure?"

He pauses for a few seconds. Then smiles, nods. "Yeah. It's gonna be fine. Come on."

I start the horrible plunge into a black pit of terror, but I'm trying not to put it into those words in my mind. The muscles in my legs are bouncing, and I have the distinct feeling I'm going to fall forward and make a horrible racket. One step after another we descend. The darkness thickens; I feel like I'm breathing it in and it's making the air colder. There are at least twenty steps.

At the bottom of the stairway there's two doors. The one to the left is slightly ajar. I can hear the humming of the Underground Transportation System. It seems to grow louder to the right, behind the door that is closed.

Germy reaches the landing and pauses. Listens at the right door, then the left. A few seconds later he pushes the left door open and walks in! I gasp and follow him. I see five figures standing around a metal table half a second after I step past the threshold. *Five*.

There stands Chloe . . . our Chloe, between Benjamin and Dekker, hand on her head, brow furrowed. I smile when I see her, my terror forgotten. I want to rush over and hug her, but then I remember the whole reason Germy and I have come. I open my mouth, but Germy's already talking.

"We need to leave. Right now."

Dekker doesn't hesitate. "All right. Let's go."

"What?" Chloe looks at me like she's trying to make out my features.

Dekker puts his arm under one of hers and starts toward the door.

"What happened?" Jaxon asks Germy and me.

"Joseph. Like five minutes after you guys left, he said not to come here," Germy answers, heading toward the door. "Someone's on their way to check Chloe, and he sounds like bad news."

At that exact moment, like in a movie, I hear the other door opening. The familiar sound of an industrial metal door handle, and the sound of well-oiled hinges swinging wide.

SIXTEEN

Petrov's Search

We. Are. So. Dead.

I can't breathe. I can't think. I can't move. Thankfully, someone moves me.

But it barely matters. There's nowhere to hide and we know the man outside is going to be coming in here looking for Chloe. No one speaks anything intelligible; any words I can make out are terrified swear words from Allen and Jaxon as they frantically look for anywhere to hide. But there's nowhere. We can't even put Chloe back in the tiny, barely cold freezer and hope he thinks she's dead because he won't. She's awake. She won't look or feel dead.

I clamp my hand over my mouth and suck in a soblike breath through my fingers. I'm being crushed by five other bodies, helpless in a corner. We aren't the slightest bit concealed, and we have no weapons, although one look at Jaxon might convince someone otherwise. He looks like he would probably kill anyone who walks through that door.

I just pray whoever it is doesn't have a gun.

I just pray. Over and over, the same prayer:

God, hide us, please. Don't let him see us, God, I beg you.

I'm muttering the words through my fingers, almost

audibly, and I feel tears falling down my face. I hear footsteps and almost fall apart. Benjamin presses his hand over my mouth and I'm actually grateful for it. I peer around, trying to see in the dim light. Then I realize there's a figure standing behind the door. I breathe in. It's Dekker.

The door swings open silently, half concealing Dekker behind it. I can barely make him out. My breath catches in my throat when another figure steps in the room. He seems to take one step per every five of my too-rapid heartbeats. No one breathes.

Light flashes in my eyes as the lone figure aims a flashlight.

I hear someone shout, but I can't see. No words, just shouting. I blink, trying to clear my eyes, and can see the flashlight fall to the ground. I hear sounds of a struggle and then a very loud bang.

I scream.

But it wasn't a gunshot.

"We need to go. Right now." The command is from Dekker.

Benjamin pulls his hand from my mouth and starts dragging me forward. "What was the bang?" he asks.

"I hit his head on the table," Dekker says, bending down and picking up the flashlight. Shines it at each of us. "You guys OK?"

"Yeah. Does he have a gun?" Allen asks this from somewhere to my right.

Dekker shines the light at the man facedown on the floor. Bends down and retrieves a gun. I swallow back a sick feeling at the sight of it.

"We should keep the weapons we took from the guards outside," Jaxon says. Dekker shines the light at him. "We don't know when we could need them. And we certainly don't want them to have them," Jaxon says, tipping his chin at the figure on the floor.

"I agree," Dekker says, nodding. "But this guy's gonna wake

up, so we need to go." He puts the gun in his belt and walks through the doorway. I feel Benjamin's hand pulling me forward. I don't need him to, but he does it anyway. I can't see much, but I turn and see Jaxon helping Chloe out the door. When we reach the top of the stairs, we start running. I hear Chloe muttering softly behind me.

Benjamin finally lets go of me. When we get to the front door, I can hear voices shouting. "That's just the guards," Benjamin explains. "They're all handcuffed."

But they're shouting. And they'll alert the other officials to this scene. We head straight for the alley Germy and I came from. We don't stop except to check corners, and we hug walls the entire way.

When we finally get back to Kelly's, we open the door and shut it again as soon as possible, praying Joseph has us covered.

"What happened?" Half a dozen voices fire this question our way as soon as we get inside.

"Was the door covered?" Dekker demands, heading straight for the computer and Eli, who has just stood up from behind it.

"Yes. Yes, the door was covered. Uhh . . . according to Joseph," Eli says, and he seems to be stuck in that awkward moment between sitting and standing.

"OK," Dekker says through an exhale, then turns. "Is everyone inside?"

"Yeah," I say at the same time as four others.

"Where . . . where are we?" Chloe asks.

I turn to her, a smile finally and unexpectedly splitting my face. "We're at a friend's house. You're gonna be OK."

She has blood all over the side of her face and matted into her short brown hair.

"Is that real?" I ask Varya, motioning toward Chloe's face and head.

"Yeah, but it looks worse than it is," Varya says.

"OK." I give my attention back to Chloe, whose big brown eyes travel slowly, like a spoon stirring through pudding. "Why don't you sit down, OK?"

She knits her brow. "I told you not to come."

It takes me a second to remember what she's talking about; we're all still quite foggy. "Yeah. You did."

"And it's so dark. And freezing."

She's just rambling, but also looks at me like she wants me to explain. "Yeah, it is," is all I can say.

"And I told you not to come," she says again, only this time louder. She's clearly getting upset.

"We didn't come. You've been half frozen in a coma for about a week now." I try to explain. But she's not listening. She's already on to the next thing.

"It's so cold outside. It's freezing. I'm freezing," Chloe says, standing in the center of the room, turning slowly, looking at each person's face, searching them. "Who's that?" she asks, pointing at Jaxon. "And that?" She points to Kelly. She staggers slightly, looking around the whole house. "What is this?"

"Chloe!" Lydia's voice. She rushes over and hugs her. Pulls away when Chloe doesn't react. "You remember me, right?" Lydia says, smiling.

"Of course I remember," Chloe says.

Lydia chuckles a little despite the coldness she is feeling—we all are feeling—from Chloe. "You need to go upstairs and clean up, yeah?"

"Uh, yes," Chloe says, slowly. "I have . . . blood on me."

"Yep. But you're OK. You just need to wash it off." Lydia puts an arm around her and leads her to the stairs. She smiles over her shoulder at us before starting up the stairs.

We all exhale heavily, and the guys start unloading various weapons onto the dining room table, five of which are handguns—loaded. Dekker sits down heavily, opens and closes his right hand a few times.

"Who was that guy?" Dekker asks, looking to Germy, who stands across the table from him.

Germy shrugs. "Joseph hasn't said. Some trial patient."

"Genesis?" Dekker asks.

Germy shrugs again. "Probably."

"Eli . . . " This is all Dekker has to say.

"I'm asking him." Eli sits back, looks at the screen for about three seconds. "Uhh . . . he said . . . " Eli is reading. "Subject is Ryan Watson . . . Genesis Serum Patient Zero-Zero-One." He looks up.

Dekker nods. Looks from Eli to Germy. "Have you talked to Joseph about the plan?"

"Sorta," Germy replies. "We didn't tell him much, but from what we *did* tell him about clearing our files . . . He says it could work, but it's gonna be crazy."

"And we're, uhh . . . " Eli says, ever pausing, ever stumbling over his words. "Still running a risk of just being recognized. . . . We can deal with the facial recognition software, but it's the human guards that could be the problem."

"Yeah," Germy says, blinking a few times. "Most of us aren't very distinct but . . . some of us are." He swallows.

Dekker looks at him for a second, then nods. "You mean me."

"Yes," he says. "You and Varya especially. Since she is the president's sister."

"OK." Dekker sighs and rubs his forehead. "OK. We'll get to that, but we can't worry about it right now." His voice is heavy with stress. He lets his hand fall to the table, then looks up. "When that guy wakes up, which he probably already has, he's gonna report that someone stole Allison's body, or that she wasn't dead. And when he does that they're gonna know it's us. And, unless they *haven't* blown up all five facilities already, they'll assume we're hiding in the city—and they'll be searching for us."

Jaxon curses under his breath, drags his hands through his hair. Lets out a breath in a huff. "OK, so what do we do?"

Dekker leans forward, puts his head in his hands for several seconds, then looks up. "I'm open to suggestions, Jaxon." He leans back in the chair, rubs his collarbone hard. "If we can get access to the security cameras on the street, we can know when they're coming and how to avoid them, but there's too many of us—plus Chloe and Varya are incapacitated."

"Not to mention Kuri," Jaxon says.

"Right," Dekker says. Another heavy sigh.

"We could go to the Capitol," Sha says. I turn to see her beside Eli, who has looked up from the computer.

"We'd have access to the UTS," I put in.

"Yeah, but that can be remotely accessed and have course changes inputted from a separate server," Germy says. "Basically, they could redirect us to Russia and have us trapped. Plus, the pods fit, I think, like only four."

"We should ask Joseph," Jaxon says, simply.

"Yes, but we're trusting him with a lot now," Dekker says, scratching his head in thought.

"I know. I don't like it either, but we can't just sit here," Jaxon says, unfolding his arms and pacing. He groans. "Joseph could know of something . . . something we could do or somewhere we could go."

That's met with silence. Some of us are lost in thought, the rest of us just seem clueless. We're sitting ducks here. Just waiting for some mindless, rewritten soldier or a Genesis trial patient to come find us and haul us all away.

We have brilliant minds in this room, but those only stretch so far.

Jaxon looks at each of us. "There has to be something."

*****

"There has to be *something* you can do." Ryan's face boasts a black eye that spreads from a cut at his left eyebrow down to his cheekbone.

"Yes, there is. We're working on it," Petrov says, drumming his fingers rapidly on the desk and looking straight into the computer screen at Ryan's face. "You're sure it was Myrus?"

"Yes. And he was with six other people. I didn't get a good look at anyone but him."

"And he knocked you out, took your weapon, and fled the scene?" Petrov asks, repeating what Ryan had reported earlier.

"Yes, sir," Ryan says. "Two guards say they saw them headed west but lost visual when they entered the city."

Petrov clenches his jaw. "Ryan."

"Yes, sir?"

"You're my friend," Petrov says.

Ryan furrows his brow and swallows. "Thank you, sir."

"The Genesis serum has worked, amazingly well," Petrov says, rubbing his chin. "Your wounds. How are they?"

"I hardly notice them."

"Good," Petrov says with a nod. "You are the first to be healed by the serum. You are the first reborn of The Monarch."

Ryan blinks, but doesn't remark.

"But you are also an operative," Petrov says, enunciating his words clearly, fighting back frustration. "This was a mission . . . in which you failed."

Ryan clenches his jaw. "Yes, sir."

"You do understand that I can't make excuses for you?"

"Yes, sir. Absolutely." The screen flickers slightly, warbling Ryan's words.

"We will have whatever security footage we can salvage sent to you immediately. When you receive it, track them down and report to me."

"Yes, sir," Ryan says.

"You are permitted to kill on sight. But keeping them alive

is preferable."

"Yes, sir."

Petrov sighs. "I'll get back to you with the footage." He ends the call and leans back in his office chair.

The shutdown of the Veil compromised many street cameras and nearly all of the in-home security cameras they had access to. No one has explained yet how the virus used to cripple the dome also managed to wreak so much additional havoc. Petrov sighs deeply. If the Resistant are staying inside the city . . . they must be using one of their own homes, or the homes of people they know. He rubs his chin in deep thought. Then stands up and rushes to where Joseph has been for the past day—at least.

"Joseph!" he says, not particularly loudly, but sharply, and Joseph nearly jumps from his skin. "Sorry to bother you. I need you to do something for me."

"Oh, uhh . . . sure. What is it?" Joseph turns to face Petrov.

"I need to see a map of the city," Petrov says.

Joseph looks confused for a moment, then turns to the screen and has one pulled up within seconds. "There you are."

"OK, now have it show where each known Resistant lives," Petrov requests, leaning over Joseph's chair and looking intently at the screen. About a minute goes by, and several shapes indicating houses now glow red. "Perfect. Yes," Petrov says, victoriously. "I need security footage from those homes, or the homes near them."

Half an hour later, the search proves frivolous. None of the footage reveals anything.

Petrov sighs, defeatedly. "OK, forget that. Do you have footage from the west side of the Capitol, from about an hour ago?"

"Uhh . . . " Joseph types, and then a green night-vision video begins to play; there is no audio.

"Fast forward, slowly," Petrov says. Joseph complies and,

after no more than a few seconds, the image reveals four men entering the capitol. "OK, slow down a little more." Another second and a man and a woman enter the building. "Hmm," Petrov says. "Why would they split up?" He mutters, not really asking, just thinking aloud. Another two seconds, and seven people emerge, including the original four men helping a woman, whose features are unmistakable.

"Chloe Allison," Petrov spits out, hatred deepening his tone. She's alive. He bites his tongue to keep from lashing out.

The figures leave the frame. "Follow them," Petrov commands.

"I don't think I can keep up with them for very long, sir. Many of the cameras aren't transmitting the data they're gathering."

"I know, I know," Petrov snaps. "Just do your best."

Joseph swallows hard and searches for the next camera. The next shot reveals nothing more than the group running across the screen. The same goes for the next two cameras. Then Joseph swears. "I can't get to the next one. The strand ends here."

"All right. Get me any working cameras within . . . " Petrov pauses to think. "A thousand feet." Joseph bounces his knee as he navigates the computer. Sweat glistens on his temple. Petrov furrows his brow as he notices. "Are you all right?"

"What?" Joseph stammers. "Yeah. I'm OK."

"OK . . . " Petrov looks at him sideways, but then the cameras regain their hold on his attention.

Joseph is swiping through different views, scanning each before passing to the next.

"Stop!" Petrov lurches forward when he sees movement in one of the shots. "Replay that!"

He watches the footage for a few seconds, then smiles. "Gotcha."

SEVENTEEN

Pursuit

We're all gathered in the living room. Laura helped Varya sit up a few seconds ago, and she says she's feeling better, but walking is still looking unlikely. Chloe sits, clean after a shower, hair still wet, to the side, looking confused but occasionally asking intelligent questions. We need to do something.

Eli is having a one-sided conversation with Joseph. We haven't gotten a reply in almost an hour, and we're stressing out. Someone could pound on the door any second.

"If he answers, we can get access to the security cameras," Germy says.

"Even if he does, we shouldn't be here," Jaxon says.

"We can't move!" Zachary says. "We have Chloe, Varya, an infant, and my dad, who can't do another run like the last." His tone emphasizes the names of the four biggest concerns of the moment. "Anyways, where are we supposed to go?"

Well, there's number five.

"Anywhere but here!" Jaxon sends back, and rather loudly.

"Jaxon . . . " Paige scolds.

He exhales, nods an apology. "I'm just saying. We shouldn't sit here."

"They're just as likely to find us here as anywhere else,"

Dekker says, clearly frustrated.

"Yes, but Joseph knows where we are," Jaxon says. "He could be a liability. Now that they're looking for us, how long do we think it'll be before he decides to sell us out?"

"I know. But moving is just as risky," Dekker says, each word sharp and clear. He exhales, turns his head away. "Eli?"

"Yeah, yeah, I know. I'm still . . . hang on . . . he's replying!"

We all wait, each of us fighting the urge to walk over and watch—except for Dekker, who's looking over Eli's shoulder after about a second of gliding to a spot behind him.

"He says we . . . " Eli's face turns white, and his voice fades to simply breathing. He swallows and speaks. "He says Petrov knows we're here."

Blood drains from my face—and every face I see. Jaxon swears and walks in an agitated circle.

"And that . . . the house is sealed." Eli looks up from the computer, desperately, staring into Dekker's eyes.

No one has anything to say. We're all dumbfounded. The sound of breathing is thick, the only thing there is to hear. Jaxon says something under his breath and heads for the front door. Our eyes follow him as he crashes through the Decontamination area and makes it to the airlocked hatch. One pull on the handle, and a pit forms in my stomach.

"No," he says, pulling again.

"Jaxon, stop," Paige says, not looking at him.

Jaxon swears, then yanks again, this time with his full weight on the door.

"Jaxon!" Dekker says. He sounds angrier than I think I've ever heard him.

Jaxon takes a thick breath, breathing it out again sharply through his nose, and steps away from the door.

"Eli," Dekker says.

"He's . . . he's uhh . . . " Eli pulls himself out of the fear that has frozen the rest of us and gets lost in the computer. After a few seconds of silence the fear leaves his face, and his brow knits. "Oh . . . my." His mouth hangs open.

"What?" someone asks. My tongue is lead.

"Sha," Eli says, like he's in some kind of trance.

Sha comes from behind me and is standing behind Eli a second later. Her mouth falls open.

"Germy." Eli doesn't look away from the screen. He jerks his hand toward himself, beckoning. "Germy!"

Germy rushes past Lydia and Zachary and joins them. After a second he gains the look both Sha and Eli are wearing. "How long do we have?" Germy asks.

"An hour. Max," Eli says. "You have to do it." He gets up from the chair.

Germy sits without a word. "OK. Uhh . . . " He rests his fingers on the keys. Blinks several times. "OK." He swallows. "I can . . . access the frequency from . . . yes. I can do this. But . . . uhh . . . he needs the internal cameras. That's the only way we can do this. We have to give him the cameras in this house." He starts to type.

"What's happening?" Jaxon asks.

"Shh!" Sha, Eli, and Germy all spit this out at exactly the same time.

"Sha," Dekker says. There's no need for him to say anything more than a person's name to command their full attention.

She looks up.

"What do you need us to do?" he asks, sounding calmer than he looks.

She looks at him blankly for a few seconds. "Nothing. Nothing. There's nothing you can do. Just . . . start looking for somewhere to hide."

*****

Joseph's fingers tremble as he frantically tries to hack the necessary frequencies. Whoever he's corresponding with on the other end is much faster than he is. They already have the security cameras inside Kelly's house transmitting to this computer, and only this computer. Whoever is over there must be a genius.

Joseph's mind is exploding with the magnitude of what he just suggested to them, but it's the only way to save them. To save *her*. It's really not about any of them. But the time it could take them and the time they have can barely be stretched to match. It will be by far the most dangerous thing he's done against The Monarch to date.

He can't believe he hasn't been caught. In fact, he *doesn't* believe he hasn't been caught. Part of his mind thinks, or maybe knows, that someone has discovered him. Maybe they don't know who it is, but they know someone is messing with things. Hacking into the Genesis file was something that probably won't go unnoticed. Not to mention all the times he's accessed their files, trying to figure out how to make them clean and believable. Someone will catch on, and once they place the blame it will land on him, and he'll have nothing. It'll be all over. He'll be the next Genesis patient if he's lucky—dead if he's not.

He pushes the thought from his mind and continues to type, frantically, yet slowly, if that is possible, trying not to make a single misstep.

This is crazy. Completely impossible. Insane, actually. It'll never happen. They're all already dead. Including him. Joseph swallows back his fear—and types.

*****

"Kelly, there *has* to be somewhere!" I have her by her shoulders, but it's like she's just shut down on me. "We need to hide. Is there *anywhere* we can go?"

She's breathing fast. Probably hyperventilating. "I—I . . . I don't know."

"OK. Calm down," I say, feeling stupid for saying that at all, since it's a completely ridiculous instruction. "Breathe, OK?"

She takes a slow breath, but it's shaky. "OK. OK . . . " She swallows, her eyes darting back and forth between mine. "Uhh . . . there's . . . my closet. But there's too many clothes. . . . Umm . . . the guest room . . . has an attached bathroom? And a closet? It could work, but it's not well hidden."

"That's fine," Sha says, eyes still focusing on what Germy has been doing ceaselessly for the past five minutes. "But there has to be room for us to move. That's crucial."

"OK," I say, letting go of Kelly's shoulders. "I just need you to keep your head on, all right?"

She nods. "Yeah. OK."

"Sha, I really need to know what's going on here." It's Dekker's voice.

Sha looks at him, but then at me, because I'm staring at her. "You won't believe me. It's crazy." She looks, wide-eyed, at Dekker. "You're not gonna like it." She turns back to me. "But it's all we have."

* * * * *

Ryan has seven men behind him. His surroundings glow with the green of night vision, produced, conveniently, by the contacts he wears. The bulletproof vest that guards his torso is completely unnecessary. The Resistant don't use lethal weapons. Not these, anyway. These people he's going for are driven by a weak sense of morality, one they believe condemns killing others.

Not that he believes it's right. He just isn't going to let that stand in the way. He's minutes from the home, and he just received confirmation they haven't left. They're sitting ducks.

He can't believe he let them get away from him when he had them in the Capitol. He hadn't been on guard like he should have been, and Myrus had gotten the jump on him. He clenches his jaw and listens to the sound as his teeth grind against one another. He's lucky he's still leading these men and not following them.

His rank is undisputed. He'd been sent with Caleb Solomon and Eliza Carver, purely to make her comfortable and as a matter of convenience. Normally, the job was one given to someone less qualified. To him it had been more of a nuisance than anything. A break in the schedule. Hiccup in protocol. Whatever one wants to call it. Then he'd been shot. *One heck of a wrench.* Shot twice, which was insane. He hadn't died, though. Genesis had saved him. Even more insane.

He is walking, fully cognitive and armed to the teeth, thanks to Genesis, even though he knows the regenerative effects won't last. The healing properties are just a result of the newness of the drug to his system. Now that he is accustomed to it, even another dose won't heal him the way the first has. Not as fast, anyway. But it doesn't matter since he won't be getting shot again.

"How far out?" he asks into his radio.

"Three minutes, sir," a voice replies.

Three minutes. He wonders if they know what is coming for them. If they are prepared. If they even know they are in danger. Maybe he'll find them all asleep. The thought makes him smile. But he won't kill them.

Not all of them, anyway.

*****

"The closet. Now go!"

I'm being pushed up the stairs and then shoved alongside half a dozen other people into a closet we don't all fit in. Only the first three people are actually concealed; the rest of us can clearly see and are in full view of the rest of the room. Varya lays on the floor only about halfway concealed under the bed. The rest of the Resistant are hiding in the bathroom. Germy faces away from us, computer on a twin bed, furiously typing.

"C'mon . . . you can do it. You're so close!" Sha says, pretty loudly, right next to Germy's head.

"I know! Shut up!" he says, and I see the trembling in his hands. "I'm right there. I'm so close."

"When are they going to be here?" Jaxon asks, hushed. Beside him, Paige cradles Kuri, who's fast asleep. I breathe a silent prayer of thanks.

"Any minute," Eli breathes, standing beside Germy.

Most of us aren't even in the closet. We're just pinned between the bed and the closet doors. Anyone who walked in that door right now could see us. I close my eyes and pray hard.

God, please let this work.

Downstairs, I hear the airlocked door disengage and then slam open. My stomach vanishes. Footfalls. Someone behind me whimpers: "Oh my God, please help us." I breathe. I hear shouted words from underfoot. I clamp my hand over my mouth, try to press back farther into the closet, but to no avail. There's no more room.

"Germy," Dekker softly requests.

Germy doesn't reply. His fingers shake harder, but he types much faster. "I've got it . . . I've got it!" he says, voice hoarse. He hits several more buttons with vehemence—and then stops.

My heart is pounding out of my chest, and I try to breathe calmly, but I'm failing miserably. My whole body feels like it's trembling.

I repeat my prayer over and over. *God, please let this work.*

Someone is angrily shouting orders. I hear footsteps landing heavily on the stairs. They're almost here. They're so close.

I hear the door to Kelly's room slam open, and at least two sets of feet pound into that room. But one set continues toward us. We're exposed. I fight the urge to scream or run. I can't. I press my hand harder and harder over my mouth.

Heavy breath surrounds me. Chests expanding and contracting. The sound of tight breath through flared nostrils, each heartbeat so loud I swear I can hear it.

Another second and the door swings open, banging hard against the opposite wall. My body goes rigid, my feet meld with the floor, and then they turn to lead. My hand falls from my mouth, but it's OK because I couldn't breathe if I wanted to. We freeze, in whatever position we are in, and become as still as statues.

A man steps into the room, silver and black rifle raised. I can't see his face. Not until he turns, eyes and gun trained directly on us. His eyes move, unfocused, across our group. I watch them. I watch them because there's nothing else I can do.

I thought I couldn't breathe before. Now it's like the air has been sucked from my entire body, and my blood is drained completely. Because I'm seeing a ghost—only worse. I stare at *him*. Every feature I can see. This . . . he isn't. *He can't be.* I feel like I'm floating. Or maybe sinking. Or being ripped apart, or suffocated.

A single whisper cuts through the silence.

"Adam."

EIGHTEEN

Empty House

"Adam."

Ryan jerks around. Had he really heard that? The room is empty. The whole house is empty. The night vision effect has left the contacts since the house is fully lit. *Everyone's gone.* There should be almost twenty people hiding here, and there's nowhere they could have gone.

He *can't* have heard that. He'd just been imagining things. A strange thing to imagine, though. He takes several steps forward, peers into the closet. He steps closer. There's nothing in the closet. But it's *warm.* He leans in and it gets warmer. He lowers the rifle and steps back. It gets noticeably cooler. It almost feels like he'd just stepped away from . . . no. It can't be. The closet is empty.

He steps back, eyes darting. There is nothing here! He had just heard something. *Genesis? Is there a side effect?* He reaches out with his hand, hitting nothing but air. He comes away from the closet, raises the rifle, and clears the rest of the room. The bathroom, under the bed, and then the closet again. He blinks again and again, but there is nothing here. He stands for another second, listening.

Silence. Only the sound of his own breathing.

"Clear!" he yells and leaves the room.

There are men to his left and right, and multiple shouts of "clear!" He swings the rifle's strap over his shoulder and heads back down the stairs. The house isn't in complete disarray. It looks like they left not long ago. They must have hacked the security cameras. Looped them or something to cover their exodus. He looks around the home, examining critically. There are blankets strewn over several couches, one draped over an armchair that sits next to a TV that is still on, but muted. There are the remains of a spaghetti meal, a plausible attempt at breakfast, and . . . he opens the cupboard under the sink to find a trash can. On top: napkins and paper towels and other normal things. He grabs the can by the lip and shakes it, churning its contents.

After a second, a flash of red grabs his attention. He prods past the rest of the trash and grabs a towel with gloved hands. Blood. A lot of it. He lifts the crumpled towel from a bucket. He scrutinizes it for another second before pressing a button on his earpiece with his other hand.

"Sir?" A staticky voice.

"Hey, I got a blood sample here. Hasn't dried completely. You got the analyzer?"

"Yes, sir. Coming down the stairs."

"What's with the connection? This static is crazy," Ryan says, something like feedback ringing through his head.

"I don't know, sir. Some kind of interference."

"Weird." Ryan disconnects the intercom and breathes a sigh of relief as the aggravating noise ceases.

"Right here, sir." The man comes down the final two steps and removes the handheld blood analyzer from its case on his belt. It can identify the subject in about five minutes, less if the search is limited.

"Here." Ryan sets the rag on the counter and continues

looking through the house while the man—Parker, or Parks, or something—prepares to run the test.

Ryan wanders somewhat aimlessly into the living room. He can see there is damage to the Decontamination area, suggesting a forced entry, which means the girl who lives here, Kelly Clere, is probably still with the group. And that it's likely against her will.

Ryan stops in the living room and spins around. "Kelly Clere," he says aloud. "This house is Kelly Clere's, right?"

"Yes, sir," Parks says.

"Like *Joseph* Clere? Is she his sister or something?" Ryan asks.

"No, sir. She's his cousin, I believe," Parks says, returning to what he's doing.

Why would they come here? Ryan asks himself, not expecting an answer. And not needing one. He knows that Devynn Wildhem and Kelly Clere were associated with each other before Wildhem went off the deep end. He also knows that Joseph Clere pulled many a string to keep Wildhem in San Francisco instead of sending her to Russia. They might not have sent her there anyway. The Containment Sector is just that. Containment for those who need containing. A simple Second Class like Wildhem is hardly in need of containing.

Adam.

Ryan furrows his brow. Adam Taurine was one of the three Second Class killed in the raid on the Capitol, the one that crippled the dome because Petrov hadn't been thinking. But why he'd thought he'd heard the name by the closet upstairs he can't explain. He shrugs off the issue.

"Done yet, Parks?"

"Yes, sir," Parks says. "The blood belongs to Varya Petrov, sir."

"What?" Ryan says, walking to the kitchen counter where Parks looks into the device. "Are you sure?"

"Yes, sir. It's a definitive match," Parks says, turning the device to Ryan.

Ryan doesn't bother looking. "Run it again before I call it in."

Parks opens his mouth like he might have thought about objecting, but doesn't, takes another sample, and runs the test again.

Ryan watches but doesn't pretend to understand how the device works. About three and a half minutes later the test results are in again: *Varya Petrov.* Ryan raises his eyebrows. "All right then."

This isn't going to be a fun call.

* * * * *

"Ryan. You got them?" Petrov's voice. Hopeful.

"No, sir. There's nothing here," Ryan says, jaw clenched.

"Well, where are they?" Each word is clearly enunciated.

Ryan exhales through his nose. "I don't know, sir."

"You don't *know*?" As a rule, Petrov's patience is thin, but now it seems ready to erupt.

Ryan swallows and turns toward the front door, arms crossed.

"Anything else you have to say?" Petrov's voice is like venom.

"Yes, sir. We found a rag with blood on it. We ran the analyzer. Your sister's, sir." Ryan turns to face the television screen—one of the men had turned it off—as he waits for a reply.

"How much?"

"A lot. She's obviously injured. Probably severely."

"Any evidence that could suggest where they've gone?" Petrov asks, forcedly slow.

"None yet, sir, but I intend to continue the search."

"Hmm. All right. You'll stay there, then. But the men are not staying with you. They have other posts."

"Sir, if I could just keep one or two—"

Petrov cuts him off. "Ryan, you said yourself there is no one there. You're merely searching for clues for where they are now, since clearly the security cameras yield nothing." He stops, waits for Ryan to speak next, as if daring him to argue.

"Where will they be going, sir?"

"The Monarch has ordered the evacuation of the general populace, and we need all the help we can get." His voice is completely unyielding.

Ryan blinks a few times. "But you want me to stay here?"

"Yes. If you find anything, send it to Joseph Clere. I'll be busy the next few days. Civilians and the like." He clears his throat; he sounds starchy, cocky. "I'll check on you when I can, but for now report to Joseph. He'll keep me updated. You can use the home as a sort of base. The owner clearly isn't there, and until you find her, her house is all yours."

Ryan bites his tongue to keep from saying anything he'll regret. "Yes, sir."

Petrov ends the call.

Reporting to Joseph Clere. Ryan scoffs aloud to himself. That is completely ridiculous. He's met the kid, and wasn't impressed. Why Petrov seems to trust him so much is beyond him. Their friendship is the oddest thing Ryan has ever witnessed. The president of a Veil, who answers to no one but The Monarch himself . . . takes interest in a biology nerd? Where is the logic?

"Sir?" Parks says, and Ryan looks up, but then realizes he isn't the one being addressed. Parks is speaking into the microphone by his mouth. "Yes, sir." He glances nervously toward Ryan and starts to gather up his things. "I have orders from—"

"Yeah, I know. Get moving," Ryan snaps, brushing him off.

"Yes, sir."

The remaining six men come from various places in the house and report the same orders. Ryan treats them similarly, and after the space of about five minutes he is alone in the empty house.

He slings the rifle off his shoulder and sits down on the largest couch in the living room, looking around at the rest of the place. He takes off his gloves and leans back. That's when he notices the temperature of the couch. Ryan stands up, turns around, and places both hands, bare, on the upholstery. It is warm. Literally. Like someone had been sitting, or lying, there for hours and has only recently vacated the spot.

He stands up straight, hands at his sides, and surveys the room again. He has a terrible feeling his team has missed something crucial. He picks up the rifle again. He starts back up the stairs, regretting each step. He shouldn't go back to that closet. That would be stupid. There was nothing there, and there won't be anything there now. But he doesn't stop.

He's back in the room, standing in front of the closet, feeling ridiculous. Another check in the closet and in the bathroom reveals both to be empty. He sits defeatedly on the bed, rifle across his knees, and stares at that closet.

"Staring at an empty closet," he says into the silence after a few minutes, then chuckles at himself. He stands up, sets the rifle on the bed. It can be set to tranquilize or kill. Right now, he turns the safety on and forgets about it. He takes the earpiece out and removes the mount for the microphone from his head. He looks around the room as he undoes the Velcro straps of the bulletproof vest, lifts it off his shoulders, takes off the long-sleeved black jacket, and sets both on the bed.

He approaches the closet again, this time casually.

The eerie warmth is still there, and this time it affects him more, somehow, without the vest and long sleeves. It seems to pull back, farther into the closet, but he doesn't follow it. He looks up. Maybe a heater vent? The closet doors could keep the heat trapped. He doesn't see one immediately and doesn't have time to check again.

His vision goes fuzzy. He blinks a few times and his eyes refocus. Then it happens again. The contacts, maybe? He stands still for several seconds, and the focus is lost a few more times. Ryan can barely see during those moments, but he can hear something. It sounds like footsteps. Or the sound of moving clothing. His sight is clear again, and the sound has stopped.

Also, the warmth is gone.

NINETEEN

Introductions

It's like a game of hide-and-seek, but a million times in intensity. That feeling like, *I'm so close to the person who's about to reach out and touch me, and then all of a sudden I have to breathe because my heart is pounding, and I can feel my body straining to pull every wisp of oxygen from within me.* That feeling when your legs want to run because the adrenaline is too much, and you have to tiptoe or be found.

And in this case probably killed.

In a moment of sheer terror and suppressed panic, we escaped the closet, slipped right by him. Right by Adam. I want to cry. But I can't. I can barely breathe, so crying is out. He didn't see us—because of what Germy, Eli, Sha, and Joseph had planned as the most terrifying of last resorts I have yet to encounter. They hacked into the contacts of the men coming for us. With Joseph's help, they erased *us* from the images the men would see.

We can't risk the stairs. They could creak and give us all away. And Germy is still wrestling with the computer. I can only imagine Joseph is doing the same on his end, trying to keep us invisible, straining to do so. Something glitched. Germy confirmed he almost lost the hold on Adam's contacts, and we were almost seen. But Dekker took the chance, and while Adam struggled to see, we slipped by him.

He's . . . my heart pounds, and I won't let myself think the word. He's *alive*. He's . . . different to say the least. His eyes—there was nothing but a hardness. Something I've rarely, if ever, seen in Adam. And he seems bigger than he had been previously. He must have had some steroid injected into him, because he's only been gone . . . it can't be more than a week. The way he moved when he cleared the room suggested . . . skill. Experience. I can't fathom how they could have made him train—unless they didn't. My throat is in a knot, and my heart pumps what feels like molasses through my veins.

We're still upstairs. We'll have to go down soon, because there's nowhere to hide up here. . . . And then Adam comes out of the room, looks down the hall at us, but his eyes betray that he can't see us. I stare at him anyway. Just stare. I'm not the only one. Zachary and Lydia stare at him, and Chloe gapes at him, and at us, clearly not grasping the situation.

He turns his head left and right, then swears. "I'm losing my mind," he mutters, going back into the room for a third time. We hold our breath, but he comes out again in another few seconds, his rifle and vest now over his shoulder. He scans down the hall again, skeptical. Another second and he heads down the stairs, his steps heavy ones.

There is a collective sigh of relief, the loudest noise we've made in nearly an hour now, hidden by the pounding of Adam's feet on the stairs. I swallow back pain. I can't even process this. I had been starting to think about . . . trying to deal with . . . the fact that he was dead. And now he's alive. Impossibly, miraculously—and yet it's more of a tragedy than a miracle. Another impossible wall for him to scale. And my mind churns. Genesis is new. Maybe it can explain how he's up and walking again with, like, zero recovery time. But Germy and Eli have hardly shut up about it since we learned of it. If it's half of what it sounds like, it's almost unbeatable. I swallow heavily.

The floor shakes. It feels like an earthquake, but I know better. The Veil is collapsing, its condition ever worsening. That one felt closer than the last, but what do I know? Maybe I'm just nervous. We slip past the stairs and into Kelly's room, Dekker and Jaxon carrying Varya; they know they can't take her into the guest room. Adam has already rechecked that room.

It must have been because Chloe whispered his name. His name actually slipped across her lips before someone covered her mouth. She wasn't thinking. Like Varya said, she's disoriented. I'm not looking forward to her getting oriented, though. It's going to be hard to tell her about Adam. Maybe I won't have to.

Now we can hear him moving around downstairs. Every so often he'll make a sound. Like he turned the water on, got a drink. Turned the TV on.

We stop in Kelly's room and stand around, looking at each other with wide eyes and wide mouths. I can't explain the looks on any of the faces. Shock. Fear. Devastation. Even I can't decide whether it was worse to see Adam dead or alive in the way he is now. Zachary looks like he preferred the first.

Jaxon is the first to speak, and when he does, it's only in that nearly inaudible way that's a mix between mouthing and whispering. "We have guns."

"No." Zachary, Lydia, and I all say it in unison.

"We're not going to kill him," Dekker says, ending the matter. It's not up for discussion because . . . just, no.

"I wasn't suggesting that we *kill* him," Jaxon whispers. "All I'm saying is that he doesn't necessarily *know* we won't kill him." Jaxon looks at me as he finishes the sentence.

"We outnumber him," Germy says. "And he still can't see us."

"OK, so we stun him, knock him out, and leave," Jaxon says.

"Where would we go?" Moses says in a huff, to no one in particular, as he sits beside where Varya is lying. Moses hasn't spoken, hasn't given thought, in quite some time. It's interesting that he chooses this moment to make his objection.

Dekker looks up at Jaxon and then Germy. None of them seem to know where we could go.

"Psst." Every face looks to Eli, who made the sound. "I, well, uh . . . Kelly just got an email. Apparently they're finally evacuating the city."

Jaxon swears once again; he seems to do that a lot. "Great timing." He sighs. "So we can't go anywhere."

"No, not really," Germy says, more closely examining the email.

Dekker's eyes follow the conversation as it bounces around the room.

"What do we do about Adam?" Zachary asks, stepping toward the center of the discussion. He looks from Dekker to Jaxon a few times, but neither offers any immediate solutions. This silence holds for what seems like an entire minute or more.

"We can't keep him blind forever," Germy finally says.

"No, and he'll eventually hear us," Dekker adds. "If nothing else, we've got a baby with us." He sighs. "OK. Are you still in contact with Joseph?"

Eli looks up. "Oh, uh . . . still? No, but I can be in like two minutes." He starts typing. "What do you want me to tell him?"

Dekker rubs his forehead. "I don't know. Just tell him what's up. And where is he with our files?"

"OK." Eli waits for a reply, silence holding us for another minute or so. His eyes brighten, and he starts to read the reply. "Uhh . . . he says he's still working on the files. But that yours and Varya's are the real problems. Umm . . . he says that the person here has been given orders to report directly to him.

Not to Petrov." A sigh of relief, and he looks up. "Luck?"

"God," Lydia says, not letting a second pass.

"The *person here*?" I say, tasting the bitterness I feel. "Does he know who it is?"

Eli shrugs.

I blink away the burn of tears and nod. I'm not sure what I want. Do I want Eli to ask who it is? Or just to tell Joseph? Do I want to hear Joseph say he knew all along, just so I can hate him again? Do I want to hate him? Do I already?

"That's awesome," Jaxon says. "Let's just go knock him out and tie him up or something." He looks around, waits for someone to contest him, but this time no one does. He looks at Dekker, waiting for approval.

Dekker looks around, and no one suggests a different course of action, no one disagrees. So he shrugs. "All right, let's go."

Jaxon waves a few people behind him and Dekker, Germy confirms that Adam is still blind to them, and I swallow back a lump in my throat as they head down the stairs as softly as they can. Especially when I see the gun in Dekker's belt. I know he's not going to use it, but still . . .

Several of us, myself included, creep down the stairs a few seconds after the guys disappear. I jump when I hear the yelling start. Adam's voice, of course, is the loudest. Then there's the unmistakable thud of someone collapsing to the floor, and I come around the corner. He's down and very out.

I don't hear anything or see anything as I walk over to him and look at him. He lays awkwardly, something between facedown and on his right side. I can see part of his face, and way too much comes back. I feel my breathing quicken just as Lydia's hands slide over my shoulders and hold me close.

I can't do anything but look at him for several seconds, and then I look away. Dekker and Jaxon remove any weapons he has left on him and haul him up into a chair in which his body is very reluctant to stay. Kelly produces some ropes she had in a closet—and duct tape—and in a couple of minutes he's very secure, though not yet awake.

Kelly looks at him nervously; she's a nurse and can read vital signs. "He should wake up any second now . . . "

"What if he doesn't?" I ask.

Kelly bites her lip. "He'll wake up." Several seconds pass. "OK, how hard did you hit him?" she asks.

Jaxon looks at her, and then at him. "Why?"

"It's been a few minutes . . . "

Jaxon shrugs. "It wasn't that hard."

"What does it mean if he's not waking up?" I ask, my question a more direct one.

Kelly refixes her gaze on him. "He's probably fine."

I can't take it. I go over to him and shake his face. "Adam! Hey! Wake up!" I swallow as I remember the last time I was shaking him like this. I can almost feel every detail. "Hey. Adam!" I remember screaming. I remember exactly how that felt. I swallow back tears and keep shaking him. "Hey. Come on! Hey!" I shake his shoulders, his head lolls. I grit my teeth and slap him.

His head snaps to the left and he blinks . . . awake. I can't breathe. His eyes look around, disoriented but also acutely aware. His eyes stop on me and he blinks. There's nothing there. Nothing familiar behind them. None of that love he used to have. None of the gentleness. It's not even . . . *him*.

He looks away from me and sees Dekker. After a few seconds he utters some curse words, pulls on the restraints. They don't budge; finally he stills. He clenches his jaw angrily several times, then exhales hard through his nose. He takes several deep breaths, then cocks his head and smiles. "Dekker Myrus. Heard lots about you." He looks around, unimpressed at the rest of us.

Dekker doesn't say anything for a few seconds. He doesn't

look like he's trying to figure out what to say, but he must be. What is an appropriate response in this moment? Finally, Dekker lets slip out: "Glad to make an impression."

Adam actually chuckles at that. Reality returns. Adam looks at the group congregated around him. "Wow, there's still quite a few of you. Didn't like . . . three of your guys get killed?" He smiles at Dekker, waiting for a reaction, which he doesn't get. "Gotta hand it to you . . . you gave us all quite a shock with your little stunt. Nicely executed. But risky. You must've known someone was gonna end up dead." He licks his lips; it's a patronizing kind of movement. Direct stare at Dekker. "Pretty gutsy."

I find that most of us are also looking at Dekker, trying to see what he'll do.

"Just curious. How do you live with yourself? I mean . . . just *knowing* that you got people killed. Must really eat away at someone like you." Whoever this Adam is, he's trained. He's working hard to bait Dekker.

Dekker doesn't react, but there's a highly focused effort behind that. I want to slap Adam. I'm sure everyone does. How can he say these things? I can't even believe this is the same man. But then, of course, I remember it isn't. That stings. More than a little. In fact, it feels kinda like I got run over by a car.

Adam backs off Dekker, looks around like he's amused. "I'm still trying to figure out where you guys were hiding. Upstairs closet has a crawl space or something, right?" He smirks, turns his eyes back to me. Narrows them and thinks hard. " . . . Devynn."

My blood freezes. I didn't want this moment . . .

"Devynn, right?" He leans back in the chair as if he isn't tied and duct-taped to it. Like he's relaxing. His eyes are like steel.

I don't want to reply. Don't want to give him my name as a

weapon he can use against me. He already has my weakness in his favor. My stupid pain. But he also probably knows for a fact that Devynn is my name, and he'll *know* if I don't tell him, and *if* I don't tell him he'll try to figure out why, and if he figures out *why* then he'll realize that . . . my mind is churning.

"Devynn," I say, giving him an answer and stifling that ridiculous train of thought. "Yours?" I ask, raising my eyebrows, fighting a million urges to break down, and a dozen others to literally just hug him. Feel his breathing and his beating heart against me. But I know that's not going to do anything but make it worse, so I don't do that.

He looks at me for a long moment. A tiny, malicious smile curves the corner of his lips. "What if I said . . . Adam?"

Wow. That would hurt even if he wasn't Adam. He really has no idea how deep that just went. I smile through the anger and pain. I'm playing the actor the best I can. Swallow before replying. "Then I'd think you were a totally insensitive jerk."

He chuckles, but doesn't offer up his name. He looks away from me and back to the rest of the group.

I can see Lydia holding Zachary's hand tightly, and Zachary holding hers even tighter. Her eyes brim with tears; his stare straight at Adam, as hard as he can. I turn my eyes back, look at the man I don't know anymore. I can't fathom what they did to him to make him this way. He's so . . . dead. The way his eyes survey each of us, appraisingly . . . I just feel disgust. And pain. My eyes burn, and the lump in my throat chokes me.

"So what's your name?" Dekker demands, cocking his head as if he'd just met any person on the street.

Adam raises his eyebrows. Makes no effort to reply.

Jaxon scoffs.

We already know his name, I recall. It's Ryan . . . Watson. Or something like that. This is just a test. But there's no way he's going to tell us.

Dekker takes a step forward, looks at Adam pointedly.

Waiting, patiently. After a few seconds, he speaks. "I asked you a question."

"Noted," Adam replies, a small smile. "I see no reason to answer it."

"You think I *need* to know what your name is?" Dekker asks, folding his arms. "This is a test. Answer. Gain a little credit. Why *not* answer?"

Adam looks away, rolls his eyes like a teenager. Then takes a deep breath. "Kuri Dreal." He looks squarely at Dekker again, then zips his head toward Jaxon. Cold stare.

"Wrong answer, Ryan. Try again," Dekker says without a beat of hesitation. Did his voice waver? Probably not. But Jaxon looks like he's ready to explode. Paige isn't in the room, but if she was I'm sure that comment would completely unnerve her. Why is he doing this? Is he trying to make us all hate him?

"Ooh. 'Wrong answer, *Ryan*.' I like this. Let's keep playing this game." He settles into the chair again, unfazed, that defiant half-smile still plastered on his face.

I swallow hard. Take a deep breath.

"Remember *him*, Dekker? Remember how he *died* . . . right in front of you?" Adam presses. "How'd you *let* him die? He was, what? Seventeen? Eighteen? A kid."

"That's enough," Jaxon says through gritted teeth.

"Is it, though?" Adam comes back with a bite. "As I recall, it was . . . kinda your fault too, Jaxon. Bet your sweet little wife has a problem sleeping next to you every night knowing that."

Dekker and Jaxon are like stone. Neither move. Neither breathe. If a pin fell, Jaxon would boil over. Every muscle in him looks clenched. Then Dekker blinks and unfolds his arms. His posture relaxes, and he steps closer to Adam. "You done?"

Adam blinks.

Jaxon lets out a furious breath, but doesn't move.

Dekker steps forward again. "Are you *done*?" It's barely

a question, and I'm glad it's not directed at me. His voice is calm. Scary calm for how angry he clearly is.

Adam smiles. "Yeah. I'm done."

TWENTY

Patient 0-0-1

They left him with Myrus in the living room after another minute or two of sheer silence. The air in the room had been thick with emotions he didn't quite understand.

The way Wildhem had looked at him. The way they'd all just stared at him, barely saying anything. Demanding little or nothing. Not yelling at him for abusing the names of their dead friends. If it was just plain self-control, it was actually admirable. But what he'd experienced didn't feel like *only* that. He'd expected to be hit in the face more than once, but several of them looked like they could cry and, despite everything, he couldn't explain why this was.

Myrus hasn't said anything. In fact, he's barely moved for what must have been more than an hour.

Ryan can't see a clock, can't begin to guess what time it is. He hadn't been looking at the clock regularly even when one was available. His mind is working. There has to be a way out of this mess. But he also knows if he doesn't report soon, someone will be coming for him, so it might be best to sit tight and play it cool.

Wildhem comes down and sits on the couch opposite

Myrus. Neither man acknowledges her.

"Not talkative, are you?" she asks.

"Not particularly," Ryan replies.

"Have you told him?" she asks Myrus, turning his way.

He shakes his head.

"Do you want me to?"

"He won't believe you."

Believe what? Ryan thinks, but won't verbalize anything, of course.

"But we're not going to get anywhere by not telling him." She looks at Myrus for another few seconds—and he slowly nods.

"You've been Rewritten," Wildhem says.

Ryan blinks. "No, I haven't."

"You have. You're the Genesis trial patient, right?"

He furrows his brow. "Yes. Your point?"

"It's an advanced Rewrite serum. That's what it is," she says, eyes looking deeply into his. Searching for something.

Ryan doesn't reply. First of all, there's no way they could know about Genesis. But obviously they do—so OK, that's new. *But how?* Ryan tells himself he'll come back to that question. Second, it's *not* a Rewrite serum. And third, Petrov would have literally no good reason to Rewrite him. He raises his eyebrows, skeptical.

"You don't know who you are. You're *not* Ryan Watson. Your real name is Adam Taurine."

Ryan scoffs, laughs. "The dead guy? The one who was—"

"Shot twice in the chest. Just like you were, right?" Wildhem says, cutting him off.

He blinks. "No, he was shot in the head." But Ryan *was* shot twice in the chest. She knew that? OK. Again . . . weird.

She chuckles. "I was there. You don't think I'd remember?"

"No, you're just trying to manipulate the situation in your favor, obviously. If you can convince me that I am this dead

Adam Taurine of yours, then I won't take every chance I get to escape and kill all of you."

"Adam."

Ryan hears the name from behind him, but he can't turn to look. He remembers the voice by the closet. *This is that voice;* he's sure of it. A chill starts at the base of his spine and then stops. A woman, wrapped in a blanket, rounds the chair. Short brown hair and dark brown eyes.

Chloe Allison.

Ryan smiles. "Back from the grave."

Something's wrong with her. Her eyes bore into his head, like they're desperate for something. She looks confused, scared, like at any second she might scream. But she doesn't. She just speaks slowly. "Adam . . . "

Ryan rolls his eyes and looks away. "Nope. Wrong."

"What's wrong with him?" she asks after a beat, looking pleadingly at Myrus and Wildhem.

Another woman comes downstairs. Her face is familiar, from a file somewhere . . . some weird name with an L. She looks apologetically at Myrus and Wildhem, tries to usher Chloe from the room. But Chloe won't have it.

"What's wrong with him?" Chloe demands again, this time more loudly.

"He doesn't remember. It's all gone," Wildhem says, swallowing hard.

"He's a Second Class. It can't all be gone," Chloe insists, letting the blanket fall to the floor.

"There's nothing," Devynn says.

"He has to remember something!" This Allison—she's all worked up.

"Lydia," Myrus says calmly.

Lydia tries to get Chloe out of the room again, whispering gently, urging softly.

"Stop touching me!" Choe yells. "I've been here before with

him. This has happened *seven* times, and he's always come back. Why are you telling me there's nothing?"

Devynn stands up from the couch. "Because there is nothing! He can't remember. It's a new serum, an advanced program, and it worked, OK?" Her voice is inches from a complete yell.

Allison looks like she's about to have some kind of mental breakdown, and she presses her hands to her head. "No. *No!*"

"Lydia, can you *please* take her upstairs?" Dekker says, heavily.

Lydia takes Chloe by the shoulders. Chloe lets herself be led up the stairs.

Ryan raises his eyebrows and looks at Wildhem and Myrus. He's confused. Very confused, but refuses to let on. "You guys are going to some lengths with this charade," he says.

Myrus doesn't move, but Devynn sighs heavily. "What did they *do* to you?"

"To me?" Ryan looks at her sideways. "If they hadn't done this, I'd be dead. Pretty sure this was done *for* me. Not *to* me."

Devynn looks at him and shakes her head, tears welling in her eyes.

The whole situation is so weird. Ryan isn't sure why they aren't interrogating him or trying to use him to get out of here. Instead, they want him to believe he was once one of them. But they aren't even trying that hard. It's like they just want him to . . . trust them. There's been no effort to force him. It's making him uneasy.

They sit in silence for almost five minutes, and the air is heavy with thought. Ryan hears people moving upstairs, a few voices talking, a baby crying. His eyes fall idle on Devynn. She has rich brown hair, but it looks like she hasn't done much to it in a while. Her face is heavy with weariness; her eyes look like they've been crying. But despite that, she's not bad. She has delicate hands, a small waist, graceful neck . . . she's actually quite beautiful.

Ryan looks away from her, feels a steady throbbing at the base of his skull, rolls his neck to be rid of it. What had he been thinking about? The train of thought is gone.

The sound of feet pounding down the steps alerts all three of them. A black man, in his twenties—Zachary something-or-other—and Gerald Faltim enter the living room.

"We have footage of him in the Western Facility," Zachary says, in answer to inquisitive looks from Myrus and Wildhem.

Dekker raises his eyebrows and stands up. "Show it to him."

A half-minute later and Ryan is looking into a computer screen filled with footage from one of the four—well, five—facilities around the dome. He recognizes this one as the Western Facility because of the people in it. At first there's nothing to see, and he just looks at the screen skeptically. But then he sees what the fuss is all about.

The man talking to Chloe is *him*. Himself. *He's looking at himself.* And they are calling this man *Adam*. A wave of something terrible rushes over him. Horror? Fear? Belief? Another minute and the video ends. They all look at him, awaiting something, but he doesn't do anything.

He blinks a few times, looks at them. There's just the faintest sense of familiarity . . . the shape of Zachary's face, the color of Devynn's hair, her eyes . . .

There's a sharp pain in his head and he flinches back. A burning sensation fills the space between his ears, he clasps his hands on the arms of the chair, grits his jaw, and squeezes his eyes shut. They're saying something, but he can't hear them. Someone touches him and he opens his eyes.

"Are you all right?" It's Wildhem.

He raises his eyebrows. Confused. *What is she talking about?* Of course he's all right. "Yeah. Doing great. Just tied up here, waiting for you guys to do something." He has the distinct feeling they were talking about something, but he can't remember what. That's annoying. He shrugs her hand off his shoulder, casually so.

They all stare at him, seemingly dumbfounded.

Another few seconds and it gets really awkward. "What?" he asks, exasperated. "You just going to stare at me till I admit I'm Adam and that I'll help you escape?"

"What about the video you just saw?"

He furrows his brow. "What video?"

No one replies. They just look at each other, horrified. The silence drags on.

"Wow. You guys have really lost it, haven't you?"

*****

"What just happened?" Zachary asks.

I can't even process it. We showed him a video of himself in Chloe's facility. He had that look in his eyes . . . we were getting through to him. Then he freaked out, had some kind of . . . I don't even know. And now it's gone. He doesn't have any clue what we're talking about.

"We showed you a video a short time ago. You don't remember that?"

He raises one eyebrow, then chuckles. "You're all nuts."

I can't do anything but gape at him for another five seconds. Then I have to try something. "Show him again."

Germy restarts the video, and Adam watches, but has the same look of skepticism on his face. Then a realization: he does the same thing as before. He grips the chair with white knuckles, throws his head back. His whole body is rigid, like a seizure or intense pain. This time I don't go forward. I just stand there and watch him. Every muscle I can see—his arms, legs, hands, face—are clenched, and to the extreme. Veins bulge in his neck. Then it's like a rubber band snaps. He lets go of the chair and his body relaxes, head sagging forward. He looks directly at me, breathing heavily, but apparently seeing nothing. Then it's over.

He looks at each of us indiscriminately, posture relaxed.

We can't help but stare, and it clearly makes him uncomfortable. He once again says something snarky about all of us being completely insane, but I know that none of us are listening.

"What is this?" I say, and look at them all, just praying they have an answer, but knowing they don't.

Germy shakes his head, eyes wide, completely lost. The others look barely better. We weren't prepared for this. We knew it was worse, but this is beyond worse. *What is this?* I can't . . . *Dear God, what is this?*

It's like I can feel His pain in His answer. My eyes tear up. I swallow. "OK." I try to sound steady. Like I'm not terrified, not freaking out inside. "Germy." I look at him. "We need to talk to—" I catch myself before I say Joseph's name out loud. " . . . Eli. And we need to see what we can work out."

Germy nods. "Yeah." He closes the computer and starts up the stairs.

I start to follow him, but then look at Zachary. He looks like he's in a daze. "Zachary," I say. He looks up.

I nod for him to follow us, and he does. I can barely fathom what he's going through. I loved—no, *love*—Adam, but Zachary went through everything with him. They've known each other for longer than I've been Resistant. They've been best friends for that long. Zachary's seen him rewritten at least six times, and Adam was with him when Lydia was rewritten. They've always been there for each other, and now Adam could be worse than dead, gone forever.

I swallow away the thought as we make our way up the stairs. As we pass Kelly's room, she comes out, looks very nervous. "Hey," she says. Her mind looks like it's stretching. I admire her. I'm so glad she's here. Then, of course, I remember she can't leave. Still. She's admirable. But right now she looks strained. More so than lately, which is saying something.

"What's up?" I say, concerned.

"Varya. She has a fever."

My heart sinks. I don't have to be a doctor to know what that means. "Oh, God."

"I know. So far, it's just around one hundred degrees, but the wound is very warm, and she's . . . " Kelly sighs. "I'm doing everything I can, but she's exhibiting some very telltale signs of infection." She nods, and I can tell Kelly is done with her report, if one can call it that.

My mind is trying to think of something to say, something to suggest, something to do, but nothing comes. So I just thank her and continue in the direction I was going. We have to figure this out. Everything. Varya, Adam, all of us not dying. But I can't think. So I pray.

God, please. Help us.

TWENTY-ONE

The Contingency

Joseph reads over his message again, thinking how treasonous every word of it is.

What you're explaining is a contingency in place to support the Genesis serum. It is a reactive implant in the patient's brain that reinforces the serum in the case of blocked thought processes or deliberately closed passage in the brain reopening. In the event of something familiar to the subject before the serum triggering a reaction in his brain, the implant releases a microdose of the serum accompanied by an electric current designed to reorient the brain to the Alpha State, or the original persona created by the serum. The contingency is the strength of the serum. Without it, the serum would eventually fail -- like its predecessor.

Part of him can't help hoping they just assume he doesn't know Ryan Watson is actually Adam. He's *sure* they know, however. He can't imagine what they must be going through, especially experiencing the full effect of the contingency in that way. They cleverly avoided telling him they knew who "the patient" is, and so far he's done the same. The last thing he needs is Devynn to take control of the keyboard and turn everything into a messy emotional affair.

Disable contingency implant?

Joseph bites his lip and replies.

Not possible.
Implant transmits directly to the Headquarters in Russia.
All dosages recorded.

The argument isn't a good one. Nothing like this has stopped them so far.

Hack transmission?

He sighs. They just want him to do everything for them. Disabling the door alarms for them. Hacking contacts. Sabotaging missions. Not to mention falsifying their data onto clean files. He could be killed for *any of* this. One aspect of any action he'd taken in the past week would be worth rewriting him for and throwing him back into some basement to experiment with advanced virology, using him to find a *cure* like a complete loser.

He's not going to get caught doing this. He grits his teeth.

No. Too risky. Too many incriminating
circumstances already.

There's a long wait. He just stares at words written entirely from the depths of his own self-preservation instincts. Nothing about that sentence reflected any of the "making it right" he'd promised to do. He'd promised Devynn. Because he owes it to her. There's no reply yet, and his mind eats away at itself.

Everything he did . . . all the selfishness he will have to live with and forever regret? Every horrible torture he put her through—and he can't take this risk to make it right? To help her? He can't put himself aside for a single minute and think of just *her* for once in his life? Finally, he swallows and types a new message.

I can do it. Need time.

*****

"Any results?" I ask when Dekker comes up the stairs.

"No," he answers. "Zachary came down and told me that Varya has a fever?"

I sigh and nod. "Yeah."

He lets out a heavy breath. He looks utterly exhausted, rubs his forehead. "What does Kelly say about it?"

"Well, she said it isn't a very high fever at the moment. But that it's looking like she could have an infection."

"And she can't do anything about it?" he asks, gazing wearily at me.

"Nothing she isn't already doing," I say, holding my palms out, empty as usual. It seems like it's just one thing after another and we just have to barrel through, clueless as to what lies ahead, not even knowing how to deal with what's already here. And if we fall behind for even a second, the whole thing comes apart.

He sighs. "OK, thanks." He stands still for another second, then turns and goes into Kelly's room. I follow him. Kelly sits on the bed beside Varya.

"Hey," Varya says when we come in. "Devynn was telling me about Adam. Do you know what's up?"

Germy pipes in. "It's a chip in his head. It manipulates his brain's electrical signals and chemicals to keep him where they want him, basically. Joseph said that, theoretically, the chip is meant to activate only in emergency situations, and that's why his physical reaction is so strong. Normally there would be pretty regular therapy to keep him settled for a while before they'd put him in an environment like this."

"Oh," Varya says, a weak attempt at a smile.

"How are you feeling?" Dekker asks.

She swallows. "Pretty good, I guess." But nothing about her looks "pretty good." After a second of silent disbelief from all of us, she answers again. "Actually, I feel terrible." She blinks, but even that action looks like it takes effort.

"I'm sorry," Dekker says from behind me. "We're gonna figure this out, all right?"

She smiles. "I know you will." She nods. A beat of tense silence passes. "So . . . Adam. What are we going to do about him?"

Dekker takes a breath, looks at Germy again.

Germy answers. "Well, we're trying to see if we can hack the transmission to stop it from communicating directly with whoever's at the headquarters Joseph talked about. Once we get that, we can hopefully disable it and prevent it from stopping his memory." He finishes the sentence and smiles, a nervous, hoping-it-will-work sort of smile.

"Will it work?" Varya asks.

Germy shrugs. "Joseph said, without the chip, the serum isn't much stronger than the ones before it. But I don't know."

"Are you guys still talking with him?" Dekker asks.

"Yep," Eli says from Kelly's desk in the corner of her room. The computer was dying, so they camped out in here, I guess.

"Is it cold in here?" Varya asks. A sheen of sweat covers her brow. It's not cold. My heart sinks.

Dekker looks at her; a long second passes. "Yeah, maybe a little cold."

Kelly heads over and puts a second blanket across Varya. Then she casts me a nervous look, and I hate it. All of this. It all reeks of something terrible about to happen.

"How is Joseph doing on the identities? That definitely takes precedence over Adam, right?" Jaxon asks.

"It does," Dekker says.

"He says he's getting through it, but it's not easy," Germy says, then looks at Dekker pointedly. "It's not going to matter if someone recognizes you."

"I know," Dekker says. "I understand. I'm working through it."

*****

Joseph's phone rings, and he nearly has a heart attack. He answers it quickly. "Joseph Clere."

"This is Petrov."

Icy chills slide down from the base of his neck; he swallows hard. "Mister President, hello. How can I help you?"

"I got notified that Watson's chip activated. Have you had any problems?" His voice isn't suspicious or accusing. Just wants to know the facts.

"Oh, no. Not at all." He clears his throat. "Uhh, there were two triggers, but he reported and confirmed everything is normal."

"All right. Just wanted to make sure. He's been in frequent contact, I assume? Have you been able to access the security cameras inside the house yet?"

"He's made contact twice already." He swallows again, hoping he doesn't sound like he's making something up—which, of course, he is. "Uhh, I was working on that. But it looks like the feeds are completely dead. There must have been a surge when the dome shut down. It must have fried some cameras and not others. It's the only explanation." *OK. Partially true, but not completely.*

"All right. As long as he's reporting regularly, I'm not too concerned. Thank you, Joseph."

"You're welcome, sir."

Click.

*****

Petrov bounces his knee. Two triggers already. That means two emergencies where the Alpha State was under direct threat. His actual person was in real danger of breaking through, or the chip would not have triggered. He'd said he wasn't worried, but that isn't entirely true. He's alone in an empty house. What could possibly be a trigger? A picture of Wildhem, perhaps. He drags his hand through his hair. Of course, Ryan wouldn't know there had been a trigger after the serum did its work, but there are only so many doses the chip can release. They hadn't anticipated two triggers right off the bat.

Joseph said he is fine, but Petrov wants to speak to Ryan himself. To make sure everything is squared away. He dials Ryan's earpiece and waits.

*****

Zachary has been talking for the past fifteen minutes. Trying to reason, trying to convince, trying everything, every trick in the book, and Ryan has gotten bored. Frankly, it's exhausting watching him trying to convince him that he's Adam, when he knows for a fact that he isn't.

That's when Ryan's earpiece buzzes. Zachary is silent. They both listen as it buzzes again. "Who is that?"

Ryan shrugs.

"Dekker!" Zachary yells.

The feet pounding on the stairs are down those stairs in

only a few seconds. "What?" Dekker says, after seeing everything presumably in order.

"His earpiece is ringing," Zachary says, eyes wide.

Ryan smiles. "I gotta report, you see." He clicks his tongue. "Guess it ends here."

Dekker grabs the earpiece. "You answer this—and tell them everything is fine."

"And why would I do that?" Ryan says with a smirk.

In the next instant, Dekker has a gun pressed to his head.

"Wow. For being a peaceloving little rebel, you look like you know what to do with that thing." Ryan is smiling. Remaining totally calm.

"I do," Dekker says, voice barely more than a whisper. "Answer."

Zachary walks up and puts the earpiece to Ryan's ear, then looks at Dekker, eyes wide.

Ryan answers: "Watson."

"Ryan, this is Petrov. Just wanted to check in. Joseph says you're all right, but I wanted to talk to you myself."

"Hello, Mister President," Ryan says, grinning at Dekker.

Something flashes over Dekker's eyes. Confusion. Alarm. He'd been expecting someone else on the other end. But then it's gone, and his face is unreadable.

"How are you feeling?"

Ryan thinks hard about what he will say next. This conversation could be short. He has to make the most of it. The odds of Dekker shooting him in the head are pretty low. But the odds of Dekker *shooting him* are not as low. He has to answer. But he can't conceal them. Maybe it's worth it just to see the looks on their faces when he outright sells them out, even at gunpoint.

"Nothing's wrong. Just looking for clues," Ryan says.

Dekker doesn't relax, but neither does Zachary, which is the more alarming part. If Dekker was bluffing, Zachary would probably know it.

Petrov gives a light chuckle. "OK. Are you sure you're all right?"

"No. Nothing like that. It's all right."

There's a long silence on the line. "Ryan. What's happening?"

"No, I haven't found anyone hiding." Ryan tries to keep his expression neutral, and hopes with all he has that Petrov is catching on.

"That's good."

He's so thick, Ryan thinks. *Really not as smart as he would like me to think.* "No, nothing." He shakes his head, keeping up the facade.

"Are you feeling OK? How are your wounds?"

"No. I'm not. It's not," he says, then chuckles just a bit, like he's having a regular conversation.

"Ryan, you're not making any sense."

"I know."

"What do you mean, 'I know'?"

"It's all going according to plan." Ryan has to consciously not clench his jaw in frustration. Because he's the first of the Genesis patients, Petrov has no way of knowing this nonsensical talk isn't some weird psychosis caused by the drug. There's no way any of this is going to work.

Petrov is silent for another second.

Finally, Ryan sighs. Takes a breath. *Here goes.* "I'm being held at gunpoint. They're all here. Get everyone to converge on this address—"

Ryan's vision goes black.

TWENTY-TWO

Surrender

I hear a single, loud swear word from downstairs, and my blood chills.

"They're coming. We gotta go!" Dekker's up the stairs in just a couple of bounds. "We need an escape. Get Joseph!" he hollers to whoever is near the computer

Eli heads back to the computer, but Dekker shouts at him. "*No!* Call him! We don't have time!"

I grab Kelly's phone from her desk, dial Joseph's number from memory, and put it on speaker so I won't have to explain the conversation later.

"Who is this? And what are you thinking?"

"Joseph, it's Devynn. We need help. Adam. He sold us out. They're coming."

There's the slightest beat of silence. I decide I need to fill it immediately.

"*Right now,* Joseph!"

"All right. All right! I'm trying!"

"Hurry." Everyone stares at me, and the whole world feels like it's a string stretched to its absolute limit, just about to snap.

"What about the identities?" Dekker asks.

"They're . . . they're not completely ready," Joseph answers as we all listen. "It might work, but the odds aren't good."

Dekker grits his teeth. "Is it the best we have?"

"Uhh . . . no. No! The evacuation. There's busses. If you can get on one, I think I can cover you."

"How?" Dekker and like five others of us shout this question at the same time.

"I don't know. You'll have to trust me." He sounds strained. "OK, keep me on the line, and I can walk you through this."

"OK, but we have to go," Dekker says.

I immediately look at Varya.

Her eyes are wide and she is shivering slightly. She stares directly at Dekker, who is looking at her too, thinking. He snaps into action, grabbing the blankets and the pole we carried her over here with.

"You'll have to move fast." It's Joseph's voice through the phone. "No extra weight, and you need to leave right now. They're literally on their way."

There's a breath of silence from everyone who understands what that really means, but not Dekker. He's got the sling basically ready.

Varya swallows, speaks. "Leave me here."

Dekker doesn't hesitate. "No."

"You have to." She insists. Her voice wavers because she's shivering. "You have to go. I'm slowing you down already."

"Devynn?" Joseph's voice. But I don't answer it.

Dekker's ignoring her.

"Dekker!" Varya yells at him.

"No!" He yells back. "We can carry you. I can carry you, so we're *not* leaving you."

"Yes, you are," she says. "They don't know I'm with you. As far as my brother knows, Adam kidnapped me, you shot me, and you guys have been dragging me around everywhere. He'll trust me. I'll be fine."

Everyone focuses on these two, because what else are we going to do?

Dekker doesn't say anything.

"And if you don't leave me, I will probably die anyway." She says it with more strength than I can fathom. "I'm shot, Dekker. And you can't take care of me like this. Leave me. I'll be fine." Her words are stark, and each one seems to stand alone.

Dekker looks like he's fighting a war inside himself. He breathes heavily, and his eyes are locked on Varya's. "Oh, God," he says.

Joseph's voice: "You have to go!"

"Should I stay? Will they recognize me?" Dekker asks. I can see him grasping for any reason not to leave Varya here.

"They might, but that's not the problem! I have it figured out!" Joseph says.

"No," Varya says. "If you're still with me and I try to say that I'm loyal, they'll never buy it. You have to go."

"Dekker." Jaxon says it as calmly as he can.

Varya: "Please go."

Dekker exhales through clenched teeth. He steps forward and presses a firm kiss on Varya's forehead. He pulls away. "I'm sorry."

"I know. But don't be. Go!" She pushes him away.

Joseph again: "Go. *Now!* Or it'll be too late."

"OK, we have to go," Dekker says. He looks very angry, avoids all eye contact. He takes the steps two at a time on the way down, and we all follow him, but he yells anyway. "Let's go!"

He passes Adam, whose head is lolling on his chest, unconscious. We're leaving him. My heart aches, but I do nothing. I don't want to risk waking him. Even if that means I can't touch him. I just pray I get the chance again later . . .

Dekker stops at the front door. "Joseph! Where are we going?"

Eli is the last one down the stairs. I watch him as I wait for Joseph's reply, and realize that he has the laptop. I thank God he thought to bring that. Who knows if it can be traced back to Joseph? Not that this phone call is doing him any favors.

"Uhh . . . go out the door and turn right."

Dekker presses past several people, and when he reaches me I hand him the phone. Then he makes his way back to the front, and we're out the door heading right. The cold air greets us with sharp teeth, but this time I don't even notice it. My head is throbbing with anxiety. I follow wherever the group leads. I realize Kelly is with us, beside me, eyes wide with terror. There are spotlights set up around the city to mark the evacuation points. And there are at least four . . . no five . . . holes in the dome, several of which are at least two segments wide. The scene is eerie. The white spotlights shine directly down, and the holes in our prison let in only the faintest glimpse of hope and the cruelest slices of freezing cold.

But look what we have accomplished. It's so easy to forget this, but our actions have brought all this about.

The group turns down an alley and stops. I don't know why, and I don't ask; I just turn down the alley and stop. I can hear the faint sound of the phone, but I can't make out Joseph's voice from this distance.

"Are you *crazy*?" I hear Dekker's voice just fine, though, even though he's whispering.

I hear the distinct crackling of the phone.

Dekker: "Are you *sure*?"

A crackle.

"Psst."

We all look up. Jaxon is waving us over. We all congregate around Dekker and the phone.

"OK." Dekker pauses, takes a breath. "We need to get caught."

"*What?*" I don't know who said that, but if they hadn't, I

would have.

Joseph cuts in, and we can now all hear him over the phone: "You get caught. There aren't many officials there right now thanks to Ryan, who said you were at Kelly's. I've communicated to exactly four of them, no one else, instructing them not to tell anyone else either, that we have negotiated the terms of your surrender. And you are going to come out peacefully and will be loaded on bus number twelve."

Allen cuts in: "Yeah? And what then? Then we have at least five officials to deal with!" Allen can be such a pessimist at times. But I can't say I disagree.

"Shut up! I'm not finished!" Joseph says. "They're not coming with you! You'll only have the driver."

"Are you sure they'll fall for that?" I can't tell whose voice that was.

"They don't have to like it. They're following orders," Joseph says. "But you have to go. As soon as the officials get to Kelly's house and realize you're not there, your time is cut in half."

"OK. We're going to end the call now," Dekker says.

"OK," Joseph says. "Good luck."

Dekker hits the end-call button. "You guys ready?"

"Yeah," I say. There is a loose chorus with the other voices.

"All right." He exhales and straightens. "Let's go . . . surrender."

As we walk from the safety of the alley and inch nearer and nearer to the steady beam of light let down by the spotlight, I feel utter terror in my chest. I can hear my breath, loud and thick, can see the vapor in the cold with each exhale. My heart is hammering itself against the walls of my chest.

I can see people lined up, loading onto buses in what is a kind of calm and orderly fashion, but mostly it's just a bustling herd of sheep. Being led away to who knows where. I can see men, women, and children, elderly people, people in wheelchairs, sick people . . . everyone is here. Everyone is leaving. My breath is faster. None of them know why they're leaving. None of them know the fight we have fought. None of them understand that they're not living. Their lives are lies. Everything they know is false. *And I was one of them.*

I'm only free thanks to God. Yeshua my Savior. My Love.

And thanks to Adam.

But now I'm walking forward, just like they are. Just as I would be if I hadn't been set free. Just as I would be if I wasn't awake, and seeing and feeling with my own eyes, and knowing with my own mind and memories.

Everything I'm doing right now feels wrong. Every step feels like it's one taken terribly in the wrong direction. Every instinct I have, every fiber in me that's alive, is begging me to turn and run, but I know this is the only way to survive. And I know that survival means leaving Adam behind while his mind is ravaged by the poisonous filth of Genesis. And leaving Varya behind, wounded and possibly dying, trusting her life to the hands of God. But leaving her to the hands of our worst enemy.

It all feels wrong.

Kelly grabs my hand tightly and I hold hers just as tightly. She's my friend. Maybe not my oldest friend, but still my friend, and I love her. She's being so brave. She's following a group of people she's unfamiliar with, going to a place that could mean her death, and jumping straight into it because she trusts me. I hold her hand, try to remind myself to be strong for her.

I hear the faintest sound of a baby and look to see Paige cradling Kuri in her arms. I can't imagine the stress she must feel. I see Zachary and Lydia, shining examples of God in this dark time. They're leaving behind their friend. Their strength is awe-inspiring. I see Moses, how old and loving he is, and how hard this all has been, and yet here he is, never giving up, never complaining, not even making himself known. I swallow back a lump in my throat and stay straight, following Dekker. He doesn't waver. He hasn't throughout this entire time. I thank God for him again and again. I feel like I'm saying goodbyes on the inside to all these people. My dear friends.

Something in me wants to scream. We're surrendering! How is this right? Fear has a hold on me, so I set my eyes forward and . . . begin to pray out loud.

"Dear God, protect us as we go here into the hands of our enemies." I swallow. "We're walking into danger, God, please protect us." The spotlight's beam is getting closer. "Let this work. Let us be safe. I pray, God, for Adam, whom we all love. Free him from what is binding him in lies." I pause for a brief moment. "And I pray with all my heart for Varya. Please let her be safe. Shield her from them. Let them believe her words. Heal her wounds. God, we pray she will return to us." I feel my heart pounding still harder. "I pray for Joseph, God. Protect him, please. Let Petrov not see everything that he's done for us. Let him be spared. I pray for Dekker, who's leading us. Give him confidence and strength in you. Let us all be strong. Let us get on this bus with only one driver and pass all the checkpoints and all the guards. Let them be blind to us, please." I feel my eyes burning with tears as the spot of blinding white light begins to shine on us.

"God, we trust in you."

And we step fully into the light.

TWENTY-THREE

Bus Ride

Ryan startles, wakes to the crash of the front door being broken down. His head is throbbing. He should probably start counting the head traumas he's experienced in just the past forty-eight hours. Three so far, right?

The black-clad team is walking across the room, rifles raised. "Are you all right, sir?" one of them asks, focused, direct.

"Yes," Ryan answers. Everything is quiet. "Where are they?"

As if in reply, there's a shout from upstairs. Not one of alarm. Someone calling them.

Two men head up the stairs, and after about a minute there's a shout of "Clear!" And then: "We got someone. She's suffered a gunshot wound to the abdomen. Looks like it's been given some treatment."

She? "Who is it?" Ryan shouts. Varya Petrov's blood was in the trash can. If that's her . . . well, they didn't know if she was even alive—or if she is still on their side if she was.

"Varya Petrov," comes the reply.

Suspicion confirmed. "Alive?"

"Yes, sir."

"Call a medic." A beat. "And can one of you get me out of this chair?"

One of the men lowers his rifle, grabs a knife from his belt, and takes the time to free Ryan's hands and feet from all the ropes and duct tape. As soon as he's free, Ryan stands and heads up the stairs, where two other men, faces obscured by gas masks and bodies rendered almost identical by bulky gear, stand beside the bed—on which lies none other than Varya Petrov.

She looks terrible. "I need a doctor," she moans.

"We know," Ryan says, stepping forward to look her in the face. "The question is whether we get you one."

She rolls her eyes and coughs, coughs again, then laughs lightly at him. "If you're questioning my loyalty, I suggest you call my brother."

"We will," Ryan says, looking down at her. He's still aware of this intense throbbing in his head. "Who shot you? Was it one of the Resistant?"

"Heck, no. They don't have the guts." She says it with a scoff. "Plus, they trust me."

"What do you mean, they trust you?"

"Exactly what I said, sir." She holds defiant eye contact for two seconds. "They trust me. I let them kidnap me in the first place. You didn't know that?"

Ryan furrows his brow. "You've been playing them this whole time? And they think you're one of them? They haven't found you out?"

She laughs carefully again. "Yes, I have. Yes, they think I'm one of them. They're a hundred percent convinced of it. No, they haven't found me out. Now, can I get a doctor in here?" Her voice gets louder as she carries on.

"They're already on their way," Ryan says as he turns and heads down the stairs. "Get me Petrov."

*****

The light shines directly into our eyes. What seems like only a few seconds go by before four officials converge on us and shout at us to get on our knees with our hands above our heads. Their rifles point at everyone's face in turn. Paige has to set Kuri down on the cold grass to lift her hands, and the little boy starts crying. The bus, number twelve, pulls up and stops in front of us.

One man is going from person to person, making each stand, patting them down, and sending them onto the bus. "You. Up."

I stand while keeping my hands above my head. He pats me down, quickly and effectively. I'm glad Dekker, Jaxon, and Benjamin thought to leave their guns at the house, although part of me almost wishes they still had them.

"On the bus!" The soldier takes my shoulder and pushes me toward another man, who shoves me toward the open doors of the bus.

I see out of the corner of my eye; the first man is yanking Moses roughly to his feet. I pull myself onto the bus. As soon as I'm in, I find a seat as far back as possible, wait as everyone else is loaded, and keep my hands visible and eyes down. Laura walks the aisle and sits to my left.

The doors hiss closed after Chloe, the last to be loaded, is shoved unceremoniously up the steps. However, unlike what Joseph told us, two men stay on the bus in addition to the driver. I look nervously about at all of our faces. Looks are being passed around, words mouthed, but none of them are directed at me. I'm thankful, because I couldn't catch a single one.

The bus starts to rumble forward, gently swaying as it rolls over the grass. As it turns, I can see where we'll be exiting the dome. There is a place at the arc where a tunnel-like structure has been built, and this leads straight through the dome. At the opening of the tunnel is a checkpoint. I feel dread growing inside as the bus rolls ever closer to it.

When we get there, we stop, the brakes of the bus letting out a high-pitched squeal. The driver rolls down the window, presents an ID. "Bus Twelve."

Silence. I crane my neck for a view, and can just see the face of the man scanning the driver's identification card. He pauses, looks up. "Twelve?"

"Yes."

The man's eyes widen and he nervously looks into the back as he returns the ID to the driver. "You're clear to go."

The gate rises and we sit and wait. Then we start to drive through. As soon as we enter the tunnel, blackness covers everything. And just when it should feel stiflingly silent, the bus . . . *explodes* with action. I feel people shoot to their feet beside me, hear the sound of shoes hurrying up and down the length of the bus. I hear shouts. I hear Kuri crying. The bus jolts to a halt, pressing every ounce of my weight left. Hard. Against Laura.

I feel someone land heavily against my legs, but I don't kick because I don't know who it is. I just jump, nearly out of my skin, and try not to cry out. There's a cacophony of noise from everywhere, resounding and rebounding and boiling all together inside the bus. There's the sound of one of the soldier's rifle firing, and my entire body locks up. Several people yell or scream, and after another two or three seconds it's over. I can hear my heart pounding blood through my veins.

"Is everyone OK?" Jaxon's voice.

A groan, one that's almost more of a sigh. "I'm hit."

Whose voice was that?

"Who said that?"

"Who's hit?"

Every voice asks or is thinking the same question.

"Zachary. But I'm fine, I think. It's just a graze."

"Is anyone else hit?" That's Dekker.

"No," I reply, in a chorus, but there's no way to know who answered—and more importantly, who didn't, if anyone.

"We need to get closer to the light," Dekker says. "I can't see anything. Just don't drive all the way out."

"I'm on it." Whoever said that clearly *is* on it, because within a minute we're moving slowly forward again. I can see the light that marks the end of the tunnel, and we're not far away. I can't believe how long this tunnel is . . . Maybe the dome is thicker at the base, or maybe the tunnel leading out is just long. My heart skips a beat as it begins to dawn on me what we're really doing. We're . . . *leaving*. We're getting out! Out from the dome, the Veil. This is what we have been fighting for all along. This is everything. I stand to get a better view, but I'm not the only one with that idea, and standing does nothing to improve what I can see. What I see is the guards, and the driver, flat on the floor, Zachary holding his shoulder, Lydia trying to examine it, and Allen—of all people—driving the bus.

"Sit back down," Dekker says. He's up front, looking down at the driver on the floor.

"What is it?" Jaxon asks.

"He's shot," Dekker says, not looking up.

"Is he alive?" someone asks.

Dekker pauses before answering. "No. He isn't."

*****

Petrov: "She's what?"

"Shot, but alive, and claiming she's loyal." Ryan paces the kitchen area of Kelly Clere's house. "There's no sign of the rest of the Resistant. They must have left quickly."

"Yes. I sent the unit as soon as you called." Petrov sighs.

"It's only a matter of time before we catch them," Ryan says. "They have nowhere to go."

“I know.” A pause. “Is she OK? Varya?”

“The wound looks pretty severe, but the medic is with her now.” Ryan glances upstairs. “In fact, I think they’re bringing her down.”

“Get in a pod with her. I want you both here. You need more therapy, and she needs care.”

“Sir, I’m sure that’s unnecessary. I can send her with another escort—”

“No. As you said, they have nowhere to go that we won’t see them, so you don’t need to be there. Someone else will find them. You’re not the only one capable of bringing them in. Get *here*.” Petrov bites off the sentence, bitterly.

“Is that him?” Varya’s voice.

Ryan turns.

“Is that my brother?”

“Yes.”

Varya holds out her hand. “Lemme talk to him.”

“Hold a second, sir.” Ryan hands the earpiece over.

Varya presses the earpiece in and speaks. “Dmitri.” A pause. “Yeah, yeah, I’m fine. Listen to me. Joseph Clere is betraying you. He’s been getting information for the Resistant for the past several days. He’s why they’ve slipped by you so many times.” Another pause. “Of course I’m sure. They spoke to him right in front of me.” Her eyes move back and forth as she listens. “No. I’m telling you. They trust me *completely*. Even Myrus is drooling all over me.” A pause, and she gives a slight chuckle. “Oh, you know . . . strong beautiful female. We’re irresistible.” A pause. “That’s not important right now. *Get Joseph.* He’s probably helping them right now. They were planning to get out on one of the evac buses.” Pause. “No, I don’t know which one.” She raises her eyebrows and now speaks in a condescending tone. “Well, they’re *not* secure, because nothing in your system is secure. No, stop. Listen to me or don’t, but I’m telling you, if you don’t stop them, they’ll be out of the dome, with their own official driver and a bus at their disposal." She takes the earpiece out and holds it out to Ryan.

Ryan puts it back on. "Still want me in Russia, sir?"

"Yes. Both of you." Petrov lets out a frustrated huff. "You just need to check in, send the men with you now—other than the medic and one other—to the evacuation site. You, my sister, the medic, and one other, get on a pod. Now." The line falls silent.

Ryan grits his teeth and relays the message. In less than a minute, all but four of them have left the house. Ryan straps on the last of his gear. "All right. We're moving out." The medic, Yost, and the other officer, Brennan, carry Varya on a stretcher out the front door after Ryan. It's freezing outside, but the Capitol isn't far.

Each step carries resentment. Leaving? Going to Russia. And for what? Therapy? Ryan rolls his eyes. He belongs *here*. Tracking down the Resistant. He knows where they are, or at least has a general area. But now, with all this delay, they could be outside already. Who knows what they might do to get out? He should be here so he can stop them before they leave.

Not that it'll matter once they get out.

They have no idea what's out there. They were probably too naive to think about what the world looks like now. Maybe they just weren't sure. Maybe they're expecting some overgrown forest, or just a desert.

However, the truth is quite different. And they're not gonna like it.

TWENTY-FOUR

Nightmares

We stopped the bus just inside the mouth of the tunnel. No one moves, other than Dekker and Jaxon, who are trying to get the two living guards tightly tied and secured. They had handcuffs in their belts, so now they're wearing them. We're not dumping them out in this vicinity because they're going to be tracking this bus. If they aren't already. So we can't just escape in this vehicle. And the guards are going to start shouting as soon as they wake up. So we're going to leave them in the bus until we go. Eli and Germy are helping Sha disable whatever tracking methods might be in place. Apparently, she used to work with high-tech cars. Before she realized hacking was her thing, I guess. Either way, they're all ignoring—or doing their best to ignore—the dead man behind them.

The bullet that grazed Zachary hit the driver in the back of the neck. I hope he died instantly because, from what I can see, he bled—a lot. I don't make much of an effort to see it. I don't want to see him.

Laura is bouncing her knee beside me. "We have to go," she says.

I nod, because she's right, but also because I don't want to say anything. I don't want to open my mouth. My stomach is in knots over . . . everything. The dead man. The bus. We're being tracked. The fact that anyone could come barreling down the tunnel at any moment. But I don't do anything. I just breathe and pray.

I let my eyes close, and it's like everything melts away . . .

. . . I'm looking down into black water. The same water that drowned me before. But this time I'm not afraid. I have the feeling that I'm holding someone's hand. Yeshua's hand. I look, but I don't see Him. I look back to the water.

"Why am I here?" I ask. Am I dreaming? Hallucinating? Is this some kind of flashback, or a vision? I don't know, but it continues.

My voice echoes over the lightly rippling surface and comes back at me, but the words have changed: *"You know why you're here."*

I raise my eyebrows, and then furrow them. I don't think I know why I'm here . . . do I? I look down at the water. It's like a beach, only without sand. There's a sleek black shore sloping down into the black water that gently laps at the glassy edge. I take a step and feel the cold black glass under my feet, which are bare. I take a few more steps and my feet meet the water, which must be perfect body temperature because I barely feel when my toes get wet. I take another step, expecting the slope to continue. It doesn't.

I fall straight down into the pool, but I don't panic. I don't kick or gasp or anything. I just sink. I don't feel the need to breathe in, and I'm not holding my breath. I don't seem to be breathing at all. But it doesn't seem to matter.

My feet hit the bottom. I feel my hair tumble down across my shoulders, and then float back up again. I look around, but everything's just dark. I can see the floor stretching out, empty, around me. I hold out my hand and I can see it, even though

I don't think there's light coming from anywhere specifically.

"Anna."

I hear Petrov's voice and hold tighter to Yeshua's invisible hand.

"Don't worry," He's saying. *"Just take a deep breath."*

I obey, hear myself breathing in and then out. This must be a memory. But why right now?

Suddenly, I start to choke. Now it's like I can't breathe. I reach out for Yeshua's hand and . . . I can't feel it. I try to calm down, but my lungs are burning. I kick my feet out, and the floor I had just been standing on is gone from beneath me.

What's happening? Am I going to drown again?

The fear that I'd somehow evaded catches up now, and my heart starts to pound. I start swimming as fast as I can, but I can't even tell if I'm headed up. I get my answer when my fingers meet a smooth surface. I immediately spin and go to kick off of the surface—only to find that it's vanished. I reach out with my hands and hit another surface, but as soon as my fingers lose contact it's gone. I've gone in every direction—and hit the same smooth, glassy feeling I thought would be the bottom. It's like a bubble around me.

I suck in a huge mouthful of water and start to cough. My mind is abuzz, my throat and lungs aflame. I'm pulling the water into my body because I can't help it. Each breath burns, and none of them come close to satisfying. Finally I stop. I fall limp and the water holds me, suspended in this glass prison.

I'm going to die.

Then I'm standing a few yards from the the edge of the water again. Yeshua's hand is in mine. I look, and ahead of me I'm standing with my feet in the water. Confused, I look down, but my feet aren't touching the water. I look back up. I'm looking at myself. I watch as she . . . I take that next step and once again plunge down.

Is this a loop? I'm watching myself do what I just did a few moments ago. I stand and wait, but then get the horrid feeling that she's down there drowning and needs help. I'm drowning down there! I let go of Yeshua's hand to go after her. I get to the edge, my feet get wet, and I take the next step, fully expecting to plunge down, but I don't. I take another step, and nothing happens. It's like the endlessly deep pool is now suddenly only a few inches of water. Barely a puddle.

I bend down on my hands and knees and I can see myself, trapped at the bottom, unable to swim up. I don't understand any of what I'm seeing.

I look down at the woman's form that is and isn't me as she fights against the invisible cage around her. I watch her as she stops fighting and floats lifelessly in the water. I can see everything that happened to me happen to her, and then she's on the shore again. Like I was.

I stand up, confused, uncomprehending. I walk through the shallow water till I'm on the shore with her. I look at her, questioningly. Our eyes don't meet. She's looking over my shoulder. I turn to see Adam facing the water, stepping closer to the edge that swallowed me last time.

I shout and run to him, but there's no point. He takes another step. But he doesn't fall. I stop and stare at him, my heart in my throat.

He turns and faces me. "It's OK," he says. "We can walk over the water." He holds out his hand to me.

The distance between us melts away even though I don't take a single step forward. His eyes meet mine. Their deep and soft blue warmth cuts into my soul. I look at his outstretched hand. I'm reaching to take his hand when . . . something changes. The water around Adam's feet is changing. He looks down, face perplexed. Then the water starts to rise. At first, it rises slowly, but then it quickly swallows him. He's suspended in a bubble like I was, but this bubble hangs *over* the surface of the pool.

Dread envelopes me. A cruel laughter starts to ripple through the room. *Petrov's*. I hit the glass. Adam just looks at me. My heart is pounding painfully in my chest as I slam my fist again and again against the sphere trapping him. I want to speak, but no words come. He presses his hands against the glass and looks at me, eyes gently pleading. I stop hitting the glass and just look at him. He opens his mouth to say something, but I can't hear him. I open my mouth to speak, but it's like I'm silenced. It feels like if I could just scream or call out to him I could save him, but I can't make a single sound. The laughter covers all.

I put my hand on the glass, over his, and he smiles. Why is he smiling?! My heart is screaming. I can see the struggle within him. I can almost see how desperate his body is for air. He holds my eyes, deliberately. I see his jaw clench hard. The laughter around us intensifies.

I move my mouth to form his name, but there isn't the slightest sound. I push on the glass, just willing him to feel me, but he's not looking at me anymore. His eyes close. I can see his chest constricting, fighting to breathe. More laughter. *Louder*. I can see Adam battling against instinct. But he can't keep it at bay. Another second and he gasps in a lungful of water. His hands drift away from mine as he fights for breath. Tears streak down my face. Laughter. Loud, deep, all-consuming.

Adam is drowning. Drowning right in front of me, and there's nothing I can do . . .

. . . I open my eyes. I am on the bus.

Laura bounces her knee beside me.

"Did I fall asleep?" I ask, feeling like I must have.

She looks at me, uninvested. "I don't know. It's only been like two minutes since we talked, but I guess you could have."

The bus isn't moving; the stress level has gone way up. In

the bus, as well as in me. That dream felt way too real. I swallow and rub my face, trying not to imagine just how real it could be. Me, being rewritten, but coming out alive, able to walk over the water and not drown. But then Adam. Walking over the water only to have it rise up and swallow him so that he can't escape. For me to watch him die as . . . that horrible contingency chip poisons him.

I wipe the beginnings of tears from my eyes. "We really have to move," I say, to no one in particular, trying to divert my brain from the nightmare.

"I know, " Laura replies. "I think we're almost ready."

I shift my weight nervously and look toward the front of the bus, where I can see light coming through the end of the tunnel. I can't make out the scenery, but I haven't tried too hard. Fear restricts me. *What if it's horrendous out there? What if there's nothing?* What if we did all this fighting and won this victory with so high a cost, only to see that the only place we can survive is in the exact place we just escaped from?

"Let's get them off the bus," Jaxon says, gesturing to the unconscious guards and the dead man.

Within a minute, they're off.

"All right. Let's go." Dekker's voice.

I look up to see him facing all of us. The look on his face is one we all share. A look comprised of almost complete uncertainty, a tinge of fear, and yet complete resolve. The bus lurches forward.

*****

"Clere, meet me. As soon as possible." Click.

And that was it. And now Joseph is standing in an elevator. But if Petrov thinks he's just going to come straight into his office like a sheep to the slaughter, he has another thing coming.

There's too much. Petrov, or someone at least, has to be suspicious of him already. There's no way he's in the clear. Not to mention that right after he gets the Resistant out, Petrov suddenly wants to talk? *No way.*

Joseph's hands are shaking. He stares at the elevator number as it counts down. All he has to do is get on a pod and he can be free. Petrov will know. But this isn't worth it anymore. He tried to believe in the work The Monarch was doing. To be honest, he probably still does. But there are lines he can't cross. These people don't deserve to die. They don't deserve Genesis.

He finished their identities. Their clean files. He hopes they're able to use them, because they could be instrumental in continuing their survival once they get out. They have no idea how valuable what he has just done for them is. He's covered everything. He might have just bought their way into Tritos.

The number stops before the basement—and the door opens.

Joseph's stomach vanishes and his blood turns to ice.

Petrov stands in the open doorway. He doesn't smile. Doesn't do anything. Just stands there. The doors start to close, and Petrov stops them. "Get out."

Joseph doesn't move for a good three seconds. Then he steps out. What else is he supposed to do? Defiantly stand in the elevator and hope Petrov lets the doors close again?

As soon as he's past the threshold Petrov grabs Joseph's arm and hauls him to the stairs. He shoves him forward. "Walk."

Joseph doesn't ask why they won't be taking the elevator. In fact, he's pretty sure he knows why. He takes the first step up with the sickening feeling there's a countdown coinciding with each step. It could be ten . . . nine . . . or it could be three . . . two . . . He doesn't know, so he doesn't stop. He just keeps walking.

Petrov says nothing, but Joseph can hear him taking each step slowly, deliberately. Are there ten to go? Or only three? Joseph's heart is pounding. He can barely breathe. Every fiber in him is screaming, trying not to run.

Ten . . . nine . . . eight . . . nothing. He's shaking. Every inch of him is shaking. He can't take it. Not knowing. Not able to see. His vision blurs with tears and he fights them back. His breathing is rapid and shallow. Three . . . two . . . one . . .

"Stop."

He stops but doesn't turn around. Sheer panic careens through his body, but there's no point in running. There's nowhere he can go. When Petrov lays a hand on his shoulder, he nearly jumps out of his skin.

Petrov takes a tight breath through his nose. He exhales in an angry, disbelieving chuckle. "And to think I actually trusted you."

Raw terror rides Joseph's spine. His hands are shaking. It's like every part of him is conducting electricity.

Petrov sighs. "I told myself I wasn't going to do this." He removes his hand from Joseph's shoulder. Chuckles. "But after careful consideration . . . you're really not worth the time."

All the energy he'd been holding back snaps and Joseph spins around, but it's too late. Even as he's turning he can feel the needle piercing the skin of his neck. He grabs for it, but there's a rush of fluid, and the needle's already out. "Wh— . . . what was that?" he shouts.

Petrov doesn't reply.

A second passes and Joseph spins away, runs up the stairs, too aware that each step exerts his body and speeds the drug through his bloodstream. There's at least six flights, and at the fourth landing, he staggers. He flies through the door marked 7 and rushes past terrified, white-jacketed spectators.

He bursts into the lab. He looks to see three techs staring at him blankly. They blur slightly and return to focus. "What did he put in me?" Joseph shouts.

"Mr. Clere, wh—"

"Shut up!" The room is vibrating in his eyes. Joseph blinks, swallows. "Look at me!"

They stare, fear and concern in their eyes.

"What did he put in me?!" he yells again, louder than before.

They don't move, they just stare at him. He stares at them, trying to think of what drug would do this to him. What antidote can he use? . . . what? . . . how long does he have?

The door swings open behind him, but he doesn't turn.

"You three. Out." Petrov's voice, of course.

The three lab technicians hurry from the room in a frightened flurry.

Joseph is panting. "What—what did you . . . *what did you put in me!*" he screams. The floor pitches up. He staggers and grabs a table. A clipboard and . . . something else he should recognize go clattering to the white floor.

"Joseph. You betrayed me."

Petrov is walking closer, but Joseph does his best to ignore him. He has to think . . . *What is the drug?* What are his symptoms? Dizziness, confusion . . . Wait, what is he trying to think of?

"Dizziness, confusion . . . " His grip slides from the table and he falls to floor. "Disorientation . . . " He tries to continue the list, but his mind is slipping. Tears form in his eyes and his breathing shifts from heavy panting to jagged sobs.

Petrov's face is in his, distorted. He says something, but there are no words he can make out, no cohesion.

"Impaired vision, loss of comprehension . . . " The words he is trying to say come out slurred. "Slurred speech." Those words weren't even recognizable. He tries to repeat them: "Srr . . . svesh . . . " His mind feels like it's trying to work through syrup. Every thought requires effort, every motion is a battle.

Why is this happening? He tries to think. A word . . . drug. *Drug*. He's been drugged. Yes, that's it! Right?

The room swirls. He tries to stand, but falls and slumps against the leg of the table.

A blurred form kneels before him . . . he can't think of who it is. There's a movement and a sensation of someone touching . . . his shoulder? Or is that his forehead?

Words. Words that should make sense, but don't . . . someone's talking to him.

"I am sorry it came to this, Joseph."

Sorry? Joseph tries to repeat the word, but his tongue is like lead, and no sound comes. *Joseph?* That's his name, right? He feels tears running down his face. Feels his body shake. This is familiar . . . he's done this before, right?

He's crying.

He just can't remember why.

TWENTY-FIVE

Tritos

There's nothing out here. I'm peering through the thickly tinted windows and the only thing I see is fog over a desolate landscape. Doubt seeps into my brain. Suspicion. Then fear. What if . . . what if it all wasn't a lie? What if there really is a virus? I can hear my heart pounding, but I do nothing about it.

The bus is gripped in silence as we keep a straight course. The blank scenery whips by us. Allen isn't wasting any time. Everyone's faces are glued to the windows, however awkward the positions required to get them there.

"Dear God . . . " Allen says from up front.

"What?" I look forward and see nothing. Nothing different, anyway.

"Are you guys seeing this?" he asks.

I look up front, only to realize that the windshield he's looking through is obscured from view by a screen that probably lowered when we started driving. I try to look forward through the window I'm seated nearest, but only succeed in smudging the window.

Several people get up and try to go forward into the cabin. "Whoa, whoa, stop! Everyone can't fit up here," Germy says.

"We're trying to figure it out. There's a hologram over the windows. It's like the tech in the contacts."

"There's probably just a switch somewhere," Sha says. I can't see her over the heads crowding the area—but two seconds later it doesn't matter in the slightest.

The bus floods with light. Bright, warm, yellow and blue light. The most beautiful thing I've ever seen. I gasp and stare. The fog has vanished and, before my eyes, stretches a golden-brown flatland that extends away to meet the blue horizon. I try to look everywhere, but my view is still limited. I feel at least two people trying to creep in next to me.

"It's a city," someone says, and a few voices murmur the same thing.

"Where?" I ask, craning to see past the borders of the glass. Then I see something. Just a slight mirage on the distant horizon. A city skyline. It's so far out, but it seems to angle so that it would pass in front of us. But it *can't* be that big; it seems so huge. I turn and see that the half of us not looking through my side of the bus are staring through the windows on the other side. I see an opening and switch sides to look through it.

The skyline continues on this side as well. "What?" I say, out loud, and go back to the other side, certain I've made some kind of mistake. How can any city possibly be that big? But sure enough, the distant skyline continues on that side as well.

Finally I just head toward the front of the bus. Apparently, I was the only one with that idea, for once, and I actually get through. I'm standing in front of the passenger seat next to Sha and Eli, who are just staring like everyone else. There's a city out here.

And not just any city. This thing is massive. There are skyscrapers upon skyscrapers and the whole thing seems to be hovering. Within about a second of realizing that, I notice there's a wall around the city, and the wall blends with the turf, giving the impression that all the buildings start above the ground. The city looks like it swells in the center, so it must have a somewhat circular layout, which is why the edges fade into the distance nearer than the rest of the scenery. I can't do anything but gape.

"Oh my gosh," Lydia says, materializing beside me. "What is this?"

It's not really a question, so I don't answer, I just keep staring. That's when I realize we're on a road. And that we're almost at the city's edge.

"Dekker . . . " Allen's voice sounds nervous.

I turn and look toward Allen as Dekker approaches.

"What do I do? There's a checkpoint right there."

I see the checkpoint straight ahead.

Dekker looks ahead for a few seconds. Then he shakes his head. "I don't know." A breath. "OK. Just let me drive."

"No," Jaxon says. "If there's someone there, they might recognize you. Let me drive."

Dekker concedes.

A somewhat difficult maneuver ensues, but in about a minute Jaxon is driving. We're less than a hundred yards from the checkpoint. As we get closer, however, nothing seems to change. There's no action or motion, that we can see, to stop us. I can't see anyone.

A guard shack stands a few hundred feet from the wall, along with a chain-link fence forming a second perimeter around the city. The guard shack looks high-tech . . . there's a gate, but it's open. We pull up to the booth, but Jaxon doesn't stop. The bus crawls by it, and we all crane to look inside; it's vacant. We look at each other uncertainly as we pass through the open gate.

"What do we do?" Jaxon asks, looking back at the empty sentinel's post.

Dekker shrugs as Jaxon keeps driving toward the wall. "The tire tracks keep going."

He's right. I follow them with my eyes. They seem to head straight to the wall, even though there's nothing between us and that very large barrier. Another hundred feet or so, and we'll hit the wall.

The wall looms high above us. I try to look up, but the bus roof cuts off my view.

Jaxon halts the bus less than six feet from the wall.

A long period of silence is filled only by confused, tense glances.

Dekker stands up and leans forward. "The tracks continue." He points, says nothing else, and retakes a seat.

No one says anything in reply.

Jaxon furrows his brow and we start to roll forward again. I grab a bar along the frame of the vehicle, not sure what I'm anticipating. But even as the distance between us and the wall melts to nothing, there's no collision, no bump, no thump, nothing.

I gasp along with everyone else. The wall, which had seemed so solid, so ominous, melts away—and we drive straight through. We're in darkness now. *We're in the wall.*

"Welcome to Tritos."

I jump when the automated voice begins. Someone else screeches.

"Tritos is the Third of the Ten Cities which now make up the Union that has brought peace to the world. After a long period of testing in the life you have known, you are finally ready to be reintroduced into life as a part of this Union."

"Why did you stop?" Dekker asks.

"I didn't," Jaxon answers. "The bus stopped."

The voice continues. "The Veil was only a temporary period to ensure that you were Clean. Sickness and disorder have been eradicated here in Tritos."

"What is this?"

"Shh! Just listen."

"The Virus you were taught about is one that has been ravaging the world for decades, since the time of The Six Wars, but now we have it nearly controlled. However, the Hosts still pose a risk to the general populace. As such, the Veil was designed as a period of purification. And you are the pure ones! Those you have left behind will soon follow. Until then, you are the Newcomers. Welcome to Tritos!"

As if on cue—in fact, probably *on cue*—we exit the wall and the city emerges before us. A man in uniform approaches the bus.

"Everybody into the back," Jaxon hisses. "Be quiet."

He raps on the window and Jaxon rolls it down. "What's this?"

"Newcomers," Jaxon says, not hesitating.

"From SF? Are they Clean?"

"Yeah. Can't believe it myself," Jaxon says, casually. "Apparently they were almost ready to head out when it all went down."

The man knits his brow. "Really? Why the change in schedule?"

My stomach falls.

Jaxon shrugs. "That's above my pay grade, sir."

The man chuckles. "All right, then. To the right."

"Thank you." Jaxon rolls up the window and steers the bus to the right.

I blink. Wait . . . *what?* Just "to the right"? Nothing else?

"Are we alive?" Sha asks.

Dekker lets out a stressed sigh. "So far."

I take a large breath and sit back. My spine feels like it's a rubber band held at almost intolerable tension.

"We can't go through the Newcomer area," Eli says.

"Why not?" Sha asks.

"Because. They might . . . I don't know. They might have, uh . . . records," Eli answers. "We're not *actually* supposed to be here. Just because there was no one outside at that post, and just because the guy who put us through this way didn't confirm any details doesn't mean we'll have the same . . . the same luck again."

"He's probably right," Germy says, looking from Jaxon to Dekker. "The identities we were working on aren't ready yet, unless Joseph sent them within the last hour."

"What if he did send them?" Sha asks. "We wouldn't know, would we?"

Eli and Germy shake their heads.

Jaxon: "OK. But what if they stop us?"

Eli shrugs. "I don't know."

Dekker looks to Germy, who also shrugs.

"Moment of truth," Dekker says.

We crowd to the windows. A large sign reads "Welcome Newcomers." Jaxon slows but tries to keep going. Then someone appears. He walks over to the bus. We all cower silently in the back, praying Jaxon can get us out of this.

"Report. What are you all doing here?" the man asks.

"I've got Newcomers," Jaxon says, making every effort to sound casual.

The man looks down at a tablet. "You guys are bus twelve?"

"Yeah."

For a few seconds the man clicks the screen of the tablet. "All right. I need to make sure you all check out."

He stands there, making no effort to do anything. I'm confused. Then a blue light radiates through the bus, front to back, hitting everyone. Scanning us, it appears?

He looks down at his tablet. Scrolling. "All right. It looks like you guys are cleared, so just head through to Admission, please." He smiles and backs away, directing Jaxon forward.

We roll on.

I look at every face around me. Did that just happen? Are we here? Silence grips the entire bus. We're all still holding our collective breath.

"Looks like Joseph came through," Germy says simply, quietly.

"Thank you, God!" Lydia says, and this is one of the loudest things anyone's said in some time.

"Thank you, God," I say. Close my eyes. Exhale.

Everyone echoes the phrase; there is nervous laughter and other bewildered expressions of absolute wonder. I can't believe we're alive.

I lay my head back and just thank God, again and again. So tired . . .

The next second, I'm dreaming again . . .

His eyes won't open. The laughter is everywhere.

My heart skips a beat.

I can see Adam's chest heaving, his lungs filling again and again with water, desperate for air, each time denied. I can feel the hot tears on my cheeks. It's like I never stopped dreaming.

"Adam," I say, my voice barely more than a choked whisper, and not enough to be heard over the horrible laughter that fills every crevice of this eternal space.

His breathing slows, each pull of the water deep, heavy.

I feel my knees land hard on the watery surface at the exact moment the laughter stops. Everything stops. Adam stops fighting, stops breathing in the water. Then there's my own voice. Weeping. Taking in shaky breaths as I stare at his eerie form, floating lifelessly in an impossible orb of dark water.

Then the laughter starts once again. Starting from a low, reverberating chuckle and growing in volume and size. I look back at Adam . . . to see that he's opened his eyes! I stand up and look through the glass.

He looks at me. There is no recognition registering on his face. And then there is anger. Hatred. Everything I thought I'd never see . . . spreads over him. He's breathing now, not dying, but still suspended in the water. He hits the glass and the thud resonates through the space.

The laughter is now nearly manic.

I take a step back, tears of horror falling from my face, each one splashing emptily onto the water's surface.

He's vicious. Every part of him that I loved has been ripped away. He pounds the glass again and again, like he's desperate to destroy it. Unwilling to let it keep him from me.

God only knows what he intends to do when he breaks through it.

I take in a sobbing breath and turn my back to him, still hearing the force of his fists against the glass, now in chorus with the psychotic laughter . . . I can't take it. I curl to my knees, press my hands over my ears, and pray.

Oh, my God! Save me! Please let this end!

The noise continues, but a small voice slips through it all.

Go to him.

I furrow my brow.

Go to him. See him. Be My love for him.

I take my hands off my ears and rise. The tears obscure my vision as I turn to face him. He hasn't stopped or even lessened the ferocity of his attempts to break the glass. I walk to him, slowly, my feet creating ripples in the water, circles of water that seem to extend into eternity.

I stop a few inches from the glass and look at him.

See him.

But all I see is *hate.*

Be My love for him.

I wipe my eyes and look at him more directly. I can see his dark eyes, see the anger he feels. The hatred and the raw evil that reside behind them. But there's more. There has to be. I swallow and keep looking. The laughter is drowned in my thoughts.

Adam is gone.

Ryan is who remains. *He* is who I have to love.

The sobbing starts in my chest, but I keep looking; I don't take my eyes off him.

I see him. I do. I can see the weakness in him. The uncertainty, confusion, and fear that Petrov has instilled. The willingness to do anything. The face that tells me he's done terrible things. But the same look that tells me he hates himself for it. I can see him. He's broken. He's hurting. He's terrified.

Touch the glass.

I touch the glass.

He stops hitting the glass. He just looks at me.

. . . Petrov stops laughing.

One of my tears slips into the water, and the small sound of the drop begins to echo.

Then silence reigns.

TWENTY-SIX

Confronting the Truth

Ryan turns a corner and starts to loosen his bulletproof vest. Varya was taken to the infirmary on this floor; he's supposed to meet a therapist here. He pauses when he hears someone shouting down the hallway he was about to pass.

"If you use that on me, I swear . . . " A woman.

"It's the fastest way to heal you." That was Petrov.

The string of curse words that follows leaves no possible option than that the woman shouting them is, of course, Varya. No one else would speak that way to Petrov. "I don't care what you say it does! I know what *else* it does!"

Ryan furrows his brow and looks over his shoulder. He turns to walk down the corridor, taking him closer to the voices, making their words clearer. He walks softly.

"This wound could take weeks to heal. Genesis could heal it in forty-eight hours."

"I don't care! I'll save my memory rather than a week of your time, thank you very much!" A pause. "Did you think I'd just let you Rewrite me? *Seriously?* After everything I've done and been through *for you* . . . you're going to just take everything away from me? I don't even have words for you." Another pause. A deep sigh. "Did you think I wouldn't recognize him?"

Him? Ryan thinks. *Who?*

"Did you think I wouldn't know what you're trying to do to me?"

Petrov sighs. "I had hoped you would understand."

"Well, I don't." Varya spits the words. "And anyway, I'm no use to you . . . fried like that. I have Myrus's trust. If you take that away, you have nothing."

Another sigh. "All right then. I just wanted to make it better for you."

"Right." It's a sarcastic utterance.

"I swear that was all I wanted," Petrov reassures. Or tries.

"Yeah, well, that isn't going to work. If you can heal me in forty-eight hours and *not* Rewrite me, we're cool. But if I'm going to turn out like Adam—sorry . . . it's Ryan now, right? Well then, you can count me out."

Petrov says something else, but now it hardly matters. Ryan can't hear a word. *"Ryan now?"* He was Adam? Something inside of him cringes, like he's anticipating a blow. But no blow comes. He blinks a few times. He was . . . Adam. Adam Taurine?

His heart pounds a little harder. Varya and Petrov are still talking, but Ryan moves away from the door. He doesn't want Petrov to see him in this moment. . . . He's *Adam*? Genesis is a Rewrite program? Just as the Resistant said?

How much else have they said is true?

He hurries away from the conversation, which has quieted significantly. His mind is reeling. He keeps walking. He's almost to the therapist's office. He tries to remove the thought from his mind. But it won't go.

"Adam—sorry . . . Ryan now, right?"

It's like the phrase is on repeat in his mind.

He's about to open the door when the therapist opens it for him.

"Oh!" She looks down at a clipboard. "Ryan Watson?"

He blinks. "Yes."

"I was just looking for you. Please come in!"

He steps past her and sits in the chair nearest him. She takes the one opposite.

He answers all her questions, just like they're reflex. He keeps eye contact well, says things with inflection, not monotone, and keeps his expression pleasant but neutral. None of it is hard. In fact, he's barely sure how he answered half the questions.

"Anything unusual happen recently?" she asks, looking up. "Have you experienced any pain, especially in your head? Any blackouts or . . . hallucinations?"

Ryan blinks as the sentence unravels in his mind. *Hallucinations* . . . as in, recollections? He bites his tongue to keep from saying anything he'll regret. He makes a show of trying to remember. "Hmm . . . " He furrows his brow, looks slightly upward. "No. No, I don't think so."

She smiles and nods. "All right. I think that's all. I'm going to recommend you have a pickup dose, just to ensure your body is processing Genesis properly, but there doesn't seem to be need for a full second treatment." She stands. "You're free to go."

He nods and stands. "Thank you."

She opens the door and holds it for him; seems pleasant. "I'll communicate your results to President Petrov straightaway. Have a nice day."

The door closes behind him, and he stops smiling. He walks back the way he came, tugging at the collar of the vest over his shirt. Every step drives deeper a thorn of confusion. Uncertainty he's never experienced. A spine of treacherous suspicion and poisonous distrust.

Even if he was never Adam Taurine . . . Varya seems sure he once was, and equally as sure that Genesis is a Rewrite program. How much is the truth? Why doesn't Petrov say something? Why wouldn't he just tell him what Genesis really is—unless he had something to hide?

Ryan shakes the thought away as he heads up the stairs to where he'll be temporarily staying. After the "pickup dose," as the therapist put it . . . he'll hopefully be sent back to the Veil. Or Tritos. If the Resistant made it there.

Hopefully? He blinked at his brain's use of the word.

Before, he would have hoped to be stationed in those places in order to hunt the Resistant. Was that what he'd meant? Does he still want to hunt them?

Again, he tries to rid his mind of the thought. Again, he fails.

No matter how he tries, he can't be sure that hunting them is what he wants anymore.

He sets his jaw and keeps his pace up the stairs.

In about a minute, he's in his room. He takes off the heavy vest and sits heavily on the small bed. He goes over the therapist's final question in his mind.

"Have you experienced any pain, especially in your head? Any blackouts or . . . hallucinations?"

He lied with his answer. There has to be a reason she asked that. Pain in his head . . . he had that once. He can't remember what happened immediately before it. It was a minor ache. Like his neck was out. But he can't remember why it happened. Maybe that was nothing.

Blackouts. He thinks hard. There was the one time the Resistant insisted they'd shown him a video; he had no recollection of it. He'd thought they were insane. But maybe they really had shown him, and he'd blacked out.

Hallucinations? That part he'd answered truthfully. He can't recall any.

He runs his hands through his hair and exhales. Maybe there really is nothing. Maybe Genesis is a good thing, just like Petrov has been saying. Maybe Varya lost it a little. Maybe she's just delusional. Who knows? It doesn't matter.

He sighs. Actually, it *does* matter. But he can't think too much about it. If he wants answers he should really just ask Petrov. But even as that thought passes through his mind, something wards him away from it. If—*if*—there's any truth to what Varya was shouting about, and what he thinks the Resistant may have tried to tell him . . . well, then, he shouldn't ask Petrov.

In fact, he shouldn't ask Petrov, period. There's no one he *can* ask. No one except the Resistant. He sighs.

Hopefully he'll be sent back to the Veil. Either there or the City of Tritos.

Wherever they are is where he needs to be. Just not to hunt them or kill them.

To ask a few questions.

Hopefully he can remember the answers.

*****

My hand is still pressed to the glass, and Adam—or is it Ryan?—looks at it warily. Silence still holds the scene tightly. My tears still fall.

I'm trying to love him. With Yeshua's love. I want to love him for what he is, not for what he was. I want to love him for him. Not for myself. I can still feel my heart bleeding inside my chest, and the pain is almost enough to cripple me, but I'm standing here for him. For Adam. And for Ryan. This is Ryan.

I swallow hard. Blink away the cloudiness of tears. "Ryan," I say, trying not to feel bitterness in the taste of his name.

He blinks. Furrows his brow. Stares at my hand. Then looks into my eyes.

I want to see that he recognizes me. I want to see that he still loves me, but there's nothing left of that to see. I tighten my jaw to keep from sobbing. I press a little harder on the glass, begging him to feel my love. No. *God's* love.

He closes his eyes, puts his hands over them like he's trying to think. When he drags them away from his face, his brow is frustrated, confused. He looks at me and holds up his hand. He clenches it into a fist and then releases. A muscle in his jaw flexes. He's reaching for me. Slowly.

I keep my eyes on his, and he keeps his on mine. I keep my hand firmly on the glass as his hand inches closer and closer to the barrier. I just look at him. *Into* him. Trying to see him. Trying to make him see me.

Finally his hand reaches the glass. But at the moment of contact I realize . . .

The glass is gone.

Epilogue

"I have no abnormalities to report," the therapist says. "The Contingency seems to have worked completely. He has no recollection of the triggers."

Petrov nods. "Are you certain?"

"I am." She holds eye contact. "I recommended a pickup dose, and a second treatment shouldn't even be necessary."

Another nod. "Thank you."

She leaves the office, and Petrov leans back in his chair.

"See? Nothing to worry about. Genesis is secure." He is speaking to the computer screen.

Very good, Dmitri. And Clere?

Petrov clenches his jaw. "He's handled."

I see. And yet the Resistant still slipped through your hands?

He exhales hard, through his nose. "Yes, sir. They escaped." Anger heats his face. "I failed. Again. What more can I say? I'm doing everything I can to apprehend them."

A face appears on the screen.

Petrov's blood chills.

"Dmitri." The Monarch smiles slightly. "I can understand your frustration. What I neither understand, nor will continue to tolerate, is your complete and utter disregard for all the work I have done. Especially for you, in honor of your father."

Petrov swallows and averts his eyes.

"Look at me, boy!" the face booms.

Petrov corrects his gaze.

"They're in Tritos." A pause. A sarcastic chuckle. "Thanks to Clere. What do you think is the next step? The other domes? The other cities? How much destruction do these people have to wreak before you get it together and stop behaving like a child?"

Petrov lets out a breath trembling with anger, fights to keep his eyes on The Monarch's.

For nearly two minutes no words are exchanged. The Monarch holds eye contact with ease, and Petrov fights to maintain it.

Finally, The Monarch exhales and looks away. "I'm done hearing news of your failures. My grace and patience have been exhausted. I want you here, by tomorrow, for reset and reassignment."

"What?" Petrov can't even hold his tongue. "What? No, you can't—"

"Shut. Up. Your time is over. You had your chance, and that chance has been spent."

Each word slices deep into Petrov's bones.

"Here. Tomorrow."

Petrov's jaw aches from clenching so tightly. "Yes, sir." He says it through his teeth. He releases. "Who will be replacing me?"

The Monarch seems amused. He smirks before replying.

"Your sister, of course."

Archives of The Monarch: Book Three

Bonus Chapter from

RADICAL

ONE

"Tell me, Ms. Petrov … why did you do it?" His voice bears no accusation, only curiosity. Even as such his even tone manages to be chilling.

Varya taps her finger on the edge of the darkly upholstered chair. It has been three days since Ryan brought her here. A full day since she's been healed. As per her arrangement with Dmitri, she was able to avoid rewriting and yet gain the benefits of the Genesis serum. And here she is before the Monarch himself. A tall, well-built man of at least fifty, deep-set blue eyes and dark hair, just beginning to gray. He is here, but this is only Russia. The Monarch knows better than to meet her somewhere as high profile as Arkhein. "I wanted to be in the field with the Resistant," she responds, remembering the question.

"Why?"

She considers her answer. What will he want to hear? What won't he want to hear? She stops her thoughts and just answers. "I was young. I was angry. I hated my brother. I wanted to get back at him. Prove to him that he didn't own me," she says.

"That he hadn't beaten me."

"You'd planned to join them?" The Monarch asks, not sounding surprised.

She nods. "I had joined them before." She swallows. "But it hadn't worked out that time, and I realized it wasn't going to work a second time." She exhales. "I decided there was a better way."

"What was that?" His voice isn't loud. Isn't demanding or frightening. He just asks her and expects an honest answer.

She can't sense even the slightest tinge of unease in his voice. "You, sir."

He smiles, his eyes show interest. "You used me?"

"No. I used his *fear* of you. His need to win."

He looks impressed. "How?"

"He was blind. Arrogant," she says, factually. "He couldn't even fathom that I had it in me to betray him, let alone that I was a First Class. He believed I was loyal to him. The Resistant believed I was loyal to them. I was loyal to neither." She blinks. "But it wasn't enough. I wasn't getting anywhere like that. He was doubting me. I was playing my part too well. So I killed Allison." Then she rephrases, making quotations in the air with her fingers. "'Killed' her. After that, it really began. The Resistant thought I was loyal to Dmitri, and it reaffirmed his faith in me."

He nods, actively listening to her story. "Why did you keep her alive?"

"To regain the trust of the Resistant."

"But possibly lose Dmitri's forever?" The Monarch asks, tipping his head inquisitively.

"It was a chance I had to take," she says. "He would never have believed I was trying to play them. He would have thought I'd gone insane. They would never have believed I hadn't killed her. I planned to get her out and bring her back to them. Then I'd have their trust forever. And once I had that,

I would no longer need his."

"Why?" He blinks—but doesn't move his gaze from her.

"I didn't need him to trust me. My goal was to tear him down."

"Again: why?"

"I'm loyal to *you*." She holds his eyes. "I did it for your sake, sir." She smiles briefly, then breaks eye contact. "But also for my own. He was destroying the Veil. I wanted you to see that."

"In the hope that you would be chosen to take his place?"

"Yes," she answers, without wavering.

He chuckles. "You weren't exactly next in line."

"Yet here were are," she points out.

He nods. "Indeed. Though how you could have predicted this is a mystery to me," he admits.

She prepares to explain, but he doesn't pry.

Instead, he exhales. "So. What were the flaws you hoped to expose? A few are quite evident, but I'd like to hear your assessment."

Varya shifts and sits a little straighter, then relaxes. "He was ignorant. He sat by and watched the Second Class grow out of control."

"But that was all part of the experiment. You know that," he says, gently chiding.

"Experiment or not, it was naive," she says, curtly. She looks at him and can tell her tone is brushing the borders. "Excuse me. All I mean is that he had an imminent threat identified and did nothing about it. They were organizing a force, however small, that proved itself dangerous. He knew it would be. He did nothing. He was lax with them. I revealed that."

"I'd say you more than revealed that," The Monarch says with a smile. He pauses. "You're right. Everything you said is correct except this: without you, they might never have succeeded." He looks at her keenly, waiting to see how she'll take it.

Varya blinks. "They would have."

"Would they?" he asks, seeming surprised that she thinks so. "Yes, they were organized, but they had barely over a dozen. The circumstances lined up completely in their favor because Dmitri wanted them to. He let them play out right into his hand."

"Yes, by placing trackers on the things he expected them to steal. But he couldn't imagine they would have had the tech available to disable the Veil," she says.

"None of us could have," he points out. "So where is Dmitri's fault? Human limitation?"

She frowns. "He should have seen something bigger than a simple raid coming."

"And why is that?"

"Dekker Myrus."

"Ah. I see. The Radical," The Monarch says, seeming pleased.

"Dmitri had his experiment, letting the Resistant run around, barely checked, but when Myrus showed up …" She lifts a hand and lets it fall for emphasis. She blinks and sighs. "It was obvious. He missed it. He was an idiot. Drunk with power and dreams of invincibility."

"Perhaps." He leans back in his chair, eyes glinting but fixed on her. "But you knew what this would bring. You knew when Myrus showed up that things were moving along. Why did you let it happen?"

Varya furrows her brow. "Because unless they were allowed to succeed completely, all the credit would go to Dmitri for subduing a threat."

"You think I would have given him all the credit?"

She blinks. "I think I might have been given an honorable mention, sir." She smiles.

He chuckles. "I suppose that is the unfortunate way of things. But wouldn't that have been better overall? Look at the mess we have now." His voice isn't accusing, but his eyes are. He seems to look deeper into her as he speaks. "You made the selfish choice."

"No, sir," she says quickly. "No, I didn't."

"Why not?" he asks, speaking faster.

Varya feels like it's a race to prove her innocence. Like time is ticking lower in The Monarch's mind, and hers is running out. "The choice I made brought the entire issue to a screeching halt," she says. "What I brought about was the eventual result of my brother's weakness. All I did was speed it up to make it seen."

"So you absolve yourself of all blame?"

She shrugs. "Like we already established: they would have succeeded without me."

"And you just rode the wave." What had seemed to be accusation is slipping into an odd combination of disdain and admiration.

"Yes, sir," she says, not bragging or apologizing. She won't do either. There's no point.

There is a space of silence. Then The Monarch looks at her sideways. "You convinced Dmitri not to rewrite you by saying you had influence over Myrus. According to you, he's 'drooling all over you.'" The Monarch raises an eyebrow.

Varya swallows and chuckles to hear him using her words. "Yes, sir. I gained his trust."

He cocks his head to one side, curious. "Perhaps the feelings are mutual?"

Varya shakes her head. "No, sir. I don't trust so easily."

"Unlike Dmitri?"

"Yes." She folds her arms.

"Do you see trust as a flaw?" he asks, his voice somewhat soft, brow slightly furrowed and eyes less piercing.

She thinks hard. *What will he want to hear? No?* Finally, she's just honest. "Trust is a weakness. Isn't it, sir?"

"Maybe," he says, looking at her sympathetically. "Depends on who you ask."

"I guess so, sir," she says, suddnely confused by the whole nature of this conversation.

"Those who have been betrayed see trust as a weakness." He presses his lips together, looks at her knowingly. "Those who have never felt that pain see trust as a great strength." He shrugs. "What better thing than to have someone you can unconditionally rely on?"

"Such people don't exist, sir." She can't help but say that, no matter how bitter it sounds.

He chuckles. "Maybe not." He sighs and looks down at his hand absently. Lifts it and examines a fingernail.

She can see veins running up the back of his hand and moving in irregular lines into the sleeve of a crisp white shirt, folded up to mid-forearm. He wears no tie or jacket. He's relaxed, completely in his element. He looks strong. Highly intelligent. She can easily see why he's the leader of the entire world, even though she knows it isn't by election. The previous Monarch would have appointed him. Then, even if he'd been only a shadow of the man he is today, Varya would have made that same decision. He looks, speaks, and behaves like a powerful leader; ready to do it all himself. Alone. A Monarch.

A long moment of silence stretches between them. The Monarch looks at her and smiles. Finally, he speaks. "I don't want to underestimate you, Varya. I don't think I do," he says, his tone low and smooth. "Your ambition is … evident. And it's not something I take lightly." He pauses. "You've proven yourself excellent at manipulating trust. Including my own in Dmitri."

She doesn't reply.

"There is not a single thing you can do that will convince me you aren't working your own angle. But, I will not stand in your way as long as your interests align with mine. If they do not, I want you to know that I see you as expendable."

"Yes, sir," she answers.

"You are not invaluable," he says, in a relaxed, casual way.

It puts her on edge.

"I require restraint. You are independent. I suspect Dmitri's betrayal made you that way. I can appreciate that quality in you. But you are not free to do whatever you please. If you can't reel yourself in and be what I need you to be without regard to your self-interest, I can assure you there will not be the grace I afforded Dmitri. You opened my eyes to his weakness as well as my own. For that, I owe you thanks, but I need you to understand me, Varya. What happened in San Francisco will not happen again." His eyes are fixed on her, unblinking. "The risk you took was ill-advised and has cost the Union very much. You will find the Resistant. We will not be salvaging an entire city as well as a dome due to their influence. You are not to associate with them without my express direction. Am I clear?"

"Yes, sir," she says simply.

He exhales. "I would have you know, you have done nothing that inspires my confidence in you as trustworthy. I, for one, see trust as a strength. I want to trust you." He pauses. "But I don't." He lets that statement stand. "You're the president of the San Francisco Veil. I don't imagine that will be a pleasure. There's nothing left of it to preside over. All that remains is the test. You're proving yourself to me. By fixing this. And you will fix it." He pauses for breath. "Ian Vincent. You're familiar with him?"

"Yes, sir. The Scion."

The Scion takes up the Monarch's mantle when he reaches age sixty or if he dies unexpectedly. Every Monarch was once a Scion. However, the direction and purpose of this branch of conversation is lost on Varya.

"He'll be monitoring you in person while you carry out

the proceedings with the Resistant." He looks at her like he's gauging her response. "Just to hold everyone accountable. You answer to him now."

Varya clenches her jaw but nods. "Very well, sir."

He looks her over completely, regarding her with an expression she cannot read. He cocks his head to the side then straightens it, the mannerism making him look almost animal in his absorption. "You are not your own master." He waits for a reaction. "Do you understand?"

"Yes, sir."

He nods. "Your anger will cripple you," he says, gently. "Do you understand this?"

Varya blinks and nods. "Yes, sir."

"Your hatred for Dmitri is worthless now. Yes, it drove you. It brought you here." He takes a breath, holding eye contact. "But now you are here. You have nothing more to hate."

She doesn't voice her difference of opinion.

"When the Veil is back in working order, and the Resistant have been contained, we will see whether you are fit to be president. If you are, you will have my every blessing on your terms." He leans forward in the chair. "But until then, please consider the countless other ways there were to solve the problem Dmitri created. And don't think I've forgotten the consequences of the one you chose."

Varya opens her mouth to defend herself—but closes it again when she meets his eyes.

"I don't need an excuse. I know why you did what you did and I understand. But your motives change none of what has happened." He exhales like he's pitying her. "The Veil is irreparably damaged. The entire Third Class population could be compromised. This mess is yours as much as it was your brother's."

Varya nods. "Yes, sir."

"Tritos may be compromised."

She sighs. "Yes, sir."

"I want the Resistant rooted out. Wherever they are. The Second Class ..." He considers for a second. "Kill them if you can't capture them." He exhales through his nose. "God knows we have enough of them overrunning Russia as we speak. If you find them in Tritos, make it look clean. I don't want to cause panic."

"Yes, sir."

He thinks. Takes another breath. "I want the First Class alive, if at all feasible."

Varya nods.

"I hope we have reached an understanding," he says and rises.

She rises also. "Yes, sir. I think we have."